LOVE AT THE HOUSE PARTY

Also by Kasey Stockton

Women of Worth Series

Love in the Bargain

Love for the Spinster

Love in the Wager

Love in the Ballroom

Ladies of Devon Series

The Jewels of Halstead Manor

The Lady of Larkspur Vale

The Widow of Falbrooke Court

The Recluse of Wolfeton House

The Smuggler of Camden Cove

Stand Alone Regency Romance

To Be Loved By the Earl, Featherbottom Chronicles novella

A Duke for Lady Eve, Belles of Christmas

All is Mary and Bright, Belles of Christmas: Frost Fair

A Forgiving Heart, Seasons of Change

Contemporary Romance

Snowflake Wishes

His Stand-In Holiday Girlfriend

Snowed In on Main Street

Melodies and Mistletoe

LOVE
at the
House
Party

WOMEN OF *Worth* BOOK THREE

KASEY STOCKTON

GOLDEN OWL PRESS

For Lauren
Thank you for reading those horrible first drafts, and for believing in me.

CHAPTER 1

B acklit by the moon, the creeping dark fingers of the branches outside the attic window gave me a chill as their shadows inched closer to my feet. Dim light flickered on the walls of the small room as I pulled the quilt tighter around my shoulders. With no fire, it was all I could do to keep warm while my icy fingers threaded the thin needle again. Fighting my drooping eyelids, I focused on the final row of vines awaiting their leaves on the hem. The gown was near to finished and I was determined to complete it before I slept.

Pushing a yawn into my blanket-wrapped shoulder, I stitched another leaf. Only eight more to go.

Mr. Bancroft was nothing if not polite, and would surely compliment whatever I arrived to his house party wearing—be it a potato sack or an outdated ball gown. I chose to create something that landed in the middle. And yet, unease still skittered through my body. How was I to know I was doing the right thing?

My eyes sought the stairway. I would not fetch the letter to read again, no matter how strongly I felt the desire to reassure myself. Mr. Bancroft had stated very clearly that the house party was a mere formality—he anticipated his mother would admire me just as much as he did. All the same, he required her blessing on our union before we entered into a formal understanding. I trusted Mr. Bancroft, but the uncertainty left me feeling testy and unsettled. What if he found me very changed and regretted his desire to marry me? Until I received a proper proposal, nothing was set in stone.

The needle slipped through the muslin, pricking my finger. I shoved it into my mouth before a drop could bleed onto the fabric. This last gown was all I had left to complete, and I was not about to ruin the soft cream material due to careless fatigue.

The stitched leaves grew blurry as I made my way down the vine, completing the embroidery just before the shadows reached the tips of my toes. I tucked them farther under my chair, regardless. Draping the gown over the chest on the attic floor, I stood, pulling the blanket with me. The cold spring night wafted through cracks in the plaster walls and sent a chill down my spine. Another yawn interrupted my thoughts and I made my way from the attic, quietly creeping to the door of the bedroom I shared with my younger sister.

Pulling out the key, I unlocked the door, hoping the click and creak didn't wake my sister. The key had not always been a necessary precaution, but lately I had grown used to remaining behind locked doors—something that I was determined to change in the near future.

Slipping inside, I locked the door again and slid the bolt into place. Soft snoring punctuated the dim chamber and I watched Charlotte for a moment before settling under the quilt beside her. Doubt and anxiety crept away when my motivation lay so plainly before me. A house party was not ideal, yet neither was Mr. Bancroft. But one thing was certain: together, those two things had the ability to pull Charlotte and me from our current situation, and perhaps provide the potential to help our brother, Noah, as well.

If only he desired it.

Sighing, I rolled over, fatigue from completing four new dresses for the house party and a host of small adjustments to older gowns fully catching up with me.

"Eleanor?" a sleepy voice questioned from the other side of the bed.

"Hush, Charlotte," I whispered. "Go back to sleep."

She groaned. "You've been sewing, haven't you?"

I refused to respond. It mattered little that it was so late; I had a house party to attend. What choice did I have but to finish the gowns?

Charlotte yawned loud enough I could hear it in the thick darkness. Her voice groggy, I half wondered if she would remember this conversation in the morning. "Can we not find *some* little money to pay a seamstress?" she asked.

Squeezing my eyes shut, I shook my head, not that she could see. At seventeen, she could not quite grasp the desperation of our situation. "There is no need. I am finished now."

"You do too much," she said sleepily, already returning to the land of dreams.

"I love you, Lottie."

Another yawn interrupted her as she said, "I love you, too, sister."

Sleep failed to arrive, despite my exhausted state. I had one chance to pull my sweet sister from this horrible, bitter house and give her a chance at marriage. And I would do everything in my power to be successful.

The road to Bancroft Hill was fraught with rain. Pattering raindrops on the roof drummed a steady beat, interrupted by Emma's soft snoring opposite me in the coach. With Charlotte safely at Corden Hall in the care of our neighbor and friend,

Miss Hurst, and Noah clearly without need of a lady's maid, Emma was able to accompany me to the three-week-long house party. Her stone-like face accepted the duty with no complaint and I found myself grateful to bring a piece of home with me.

Pulling the lap rug tightly over my knees, I fought a shiver, closing my novel and tucking it away. The overcast sky had grown too dark to see clearly and reading about dreadful high-waymen with shocking facial scars was not particularly conducive to a relaxing ride along the highway, especially as I had yet to discover if the highwayman in the novel would turn out to be a blackguard or the hero. One never did know with gothic stories.

Lightning flashed in the distance, momentarily lighting the increasingly darkening carriage and I startled when Emma yelped across from me.

"It is only a storm," I soothed. "It won't be much longer to Bancroft Hill. We should be fairly close by now, I'd imagine."

She nodded, her round eyes betraying her younger years. She had only come to work for us the year prior. I had quickly promoted her to lady's maid when she'd displayed a superior talent at styling my thin, straight hair into something resembling elegance. The pale locks had long been the bane of my existence. While my hair was a lovely shade of light blonde, it was impossible to curl and rarely held a style for longer than a moment. But Emma was a master. I looked better under her care than ever before.

"Shall we play a game to pass the time?" I asked.

Emma's confused eyebrows pulled together slightly. "What sort of game?"

Before I could answer, a sudden jolt threw me from my seat. A blow reverberated through my jaw as it collided with Emma's knee, shaking both of us as the carriage shuddered to a stop.

"Mrs. Wheeler!" Emma shrieked. "Are you hurt?"

"I shall survive." Rubbing my jaw, I regained my seat. The

door flew open and rain poured sideways through the door, instantly soaking my feet through my soft leather shoes and traveling up the hem of my gown.

"Nasty storm out here, ma'am," Joe, my coachman, said.

"The roads have turned immovable?" I guessed.

His sorry face nodded. "Hit a rut back there that cracked the wheel." He closed the carriage door enough to keep out some of the rain. "A carriage has been following us for a while. I'll flag them down and ask for help."

"Thank you, Joe."

Forcing the door shut with a click, he left us in the relative warmth of the cab. I tamped down my frustration. If Noah had taken care of this carriage instead of wasting all of his money on cards and drink, I would be bouncing along to Bancroft Hill instead of slumped on the highway like a pair of discarded shoes.

Emma scooted closer to the opposite window, watching through the streams of rain. "There's it now."

"There it is now," I corrected.

She shot me a look over her shoulder, her eyebrows drawn together. "That's what I said."

It was senseless to attempt any sort of education with the girl. But at times her speech grated on me, and after raising Charlotte for the last few years, it was second nature to correct such horrid speech. "Are they stopping?"

"Yes'm. A man's talking to Joe."

"I best be part of this," I said, sighing.

"Whatever for?"

My hand rested on the door handle and I looked back at her. "Because I do not want Joe sending us with someone who isn't respectable. I'd rather wait here in the cold than ruin my reputation."

That seemed to quiet the maid. Fierce wind ripped the door from my hand and it hit the opposite side of the cab with a loud bang. I hopped down to the mud, gripping the slippery door and yanking with all of my strength, though it refused to budge.

Joe must be a man of goliath strength, for he had made it appear easy to hold the door partially open earlier.

I counted aloud, prepared to give the door one large yank with accumulated strength, "One...two...three!"

My arms flew through the air, the door coming away from the side of the carriage easily as though the wind had died down on my command. The hair whipping into my eyes said otherwise, however, and I turned to find a man standing directly behind me.

"Good heavens," I shrieked, my hand flying to my heart. "You frightened me."

"What are you doing?" he hollered over the wind. His coat was drenched, his hair plastered to his forehead.

"What business is that of yours?"

"You are heading to Bancroft Hill?" he asked, ignoring my question. His eyes narrowed at me through the pelting of icy drops of rain.

Joe. Of course my coachman would divulge this information to a complete stranger. A quite tall stranger, in fact, with hair so dark it could be black—or perhaps that was an effect of the powerful rain.

A flash lit the dark sky, giving me a glimpse of the stranger's face. He did not *appear* nefarious. His clothing screamed gentility and there were no visible scars running the length of his cheek. If he was a highwayman, he was *bound* to have scars.

"Perhaps," I replied. It was wise to be cautious. Time had already taught me that lesson.

"What?" he yelled.

I took a breath. "Perhaps!" I yelled back. The wind grew in ferocity. I suddenly realized the ridiculous nature of my circumstances, standing in a howling storm with a strange gentleman, yelling obscure answers into the rain. My gown was thoroughly soaked, hair plastered to my neck and cheeks, and my feet were glued to the mud. I was a sight, to be sure.

"I am going that direction as well. May I convey you and your maid to your destination?"

"Have you any females in your coach?" I asked.

"No." His eyes were dark against his shaded face. "Only a friend. But your maid will lend sufficient chaperonage."

I nodded, the rain making its way through every layer of clothing I wore and chilling my skin. If we did not get out of the rain right away, we were both bound to catch cold. "Lead the way, sir."

His elbow shot out, offering me an escort. I had been correct on that score, at least. He was a gentleman. I shook my head, lifting my skirts with both hands to keep them from the mud. He stood unmoving, his gaze trained on me as rain trailed down his cheeks and dripped from his straight nose.

I tried to step forward but struggled, my foot securely fastened to the mud. My balance thrown, my arms flailed, searching for purchase on the side of the slick carriage door.

Strong, cold hands came around my waist, catching me before I collided with the wet earth. Before I knew it, my legs flew into the air and I was bobbing forward. I wrapped my arms around the man's neck as he carried me around my carriage and to the doorway of his own. His heart pounded through his chest, the vibration chasing tingles down my side. I tightened my grip as the carriage door flew open, catching his eye suddenly. My cheeks warmed. He set my feet on the dry floor of his own cab and a man already seated inside reached forward to help me in.

I looked back over my shoulder and caught my stranger's stone face. Behind the mask, suppressed emotion begged release. Irritation, surely.

I moved aside to make room on the bench as my coachman ushered my maid in shortly behind me.

My toes squelched on the floor, my wet stockings sending a chill up my legs. I gasped, looking behind the man to the muddy road outside. "Sir, my shoes!"

"Are unquestionably useless," he countered, climbing inside to sit opposite me. He swung the door shut behind himself and hit the top of the carriage with his knuckles. When we failed to move, he did so again with more force, and the carriage slowly rolled forth.

"But what shall I wear?" I asked, looking behind me through the small window where my carriage sat in the mud, squat and unmoving like a sorrowful ruin. I saw my coachman climb inside to escape the rain while he waited with the carriage. It grew small in the distance then disappeared behind us. How was I going to pay for the repairs? How was I going to procure new *shoes*?

"You have only brought one pair?" he asked, one dark eyebrow arched up.

Affronted, I hardly knew what to say. "What business is that of yours?"

The men exchanged glances. Anger had caused my manners to slip and I felt a blush grow on my cheeks. I had not intended to sound so uncivil.

I would have been a simpleton not to notice that both of the men sitting opposite me were handsome, one as wet as I, the other completely dry. The dry man cleared his throat. "Perhaps we ought to introduce ourselves, given this unconventional situation. I am Mr. Andrew Peterson. This wet man is Lord Stallsbury."

Good gracious. A *lord*? And not just any lord, for his reputation preceded him. I swallowed. Being carried so intimately by a marquess known far and wide as a passionate gamester was not the correct way to guard my reputation.

They watched me expectantly and I squeezed my hands together in my lap. "A pleasure to meet you both, though I cannot say I am pleased with the circumstances. I am Mrs. Wheeler and this is my maid, Emma."

"I was unaware of a Mrs. Wheeler on the guest list," Mr. Peterson said to Lord Stallsbury. "Did Bancroft mention anything to you?"

Lord Stallsbury ran a hand over his face and through his hair, slicking water from it and spraying his friend. "I didn't ask. Though how would I when the correspondence was largely through you?"

"Excuse me," I interrupted. "Am I correct in assuming that you are traveling to Bancroft Hill on your own accord?"

"Yes," Lord Stallsbury said, the stone of his face replaced with slight irritation. I had heard many tales of his exploits in Town. If gambling did not take all of his money eventually, then drinking surely would. Word was, he was a scoundrel, and an imprudent one at that. "'Tis what I mentioned earlier."

"Oh." My conscience appeased, I relented. It appeared I was not putting them out very much at all. If one did not count the thoroughly wet bench seat and Lord Stallsbury's thoroughly wet person. But he was not the sort of man whose opinion I was overly concerned with. "And you are to attend the house party as well?"

"Yes," Lord Stallsbury confirmed.

I tried to ignore my warming cheeks. The man had only just carried me and now I was meant to attend a three-week-long house party with him. "If I may speak plainly, I would prefer it if the nature of my arrival in your carriage need not be repeated to the other guests. I can only imagine it would cause us undue discomfort."

Lord Stallsbury's searching gaze was guarded and I sallied forth. "Do not concern yourself with your actions for clearly they were necessary. I only mean that we ought to put it behind us so we might enjoy our stay at Bancroft Hill."

Silence reigned in the carriage. Perhaps the men were

unused to such candor but I could not simply leave things unsaid. I did not regret my words.

Mr. Peterson said, "It shan't be much longer before we reach the house. I'd imagine a crew of men can fetch and repair your carriage on the morrow. The ferocity of these storms never lasts more than a day or so."

Nodding, I glanced at Emma. She sat quietly on the seat beside me, the fear on her face gone. It was likely replaced with the thrill of rescue by two handsome strangers. I could not help but feel like I would have enjoyed the adventure in my youngers years, as well. But of course, I'd had enough adventure in my young life to satisfy me. I did not need any more now than I was able to glean from my novels.

No, what I needed was a nice, steady man who could lend me his name, protection, and financial security. A staid man like Mr. Bancroft.

The Mr. Bancroft who I had once nearly rejected because of the very qualities that drew me toward him now. Though we had been separated before any rejection occurred; he was never given the opportunity to offer for me then.

Shivering, I wrapped my arms around my waist, but I could not keep my teeth from chattering.

"Take this," Lord Stallsbury said, handing me a folded blanket. He gave another to Emma and then wrapped a third around his own legs. He was visibly shivering as well, and guilt pierced me for arguing with him in the rain. If this powerful lord was to become ill due to my recklessness and broken carriage, then Mrs. Bancroft would surely not be pleased. If I remembered correctly, to make Mr. Bancroft happy, the happiness of his mother was paramount.

CHAPTER 2

T he carriage plodded along, bringing us to Bancroft Hill within the hour. The house's large, square shape was like an empty fire grate, and it looked just as cold.

Lord Stallsbury eyed me with his shrewd gaze. "We must see about getting you inside quickly."

I glanced back at the house, cool and uninviting; not at all what I had imagined. "And yourself, sir. You stood in the rain longer than I." Though I could not fault his chivalry, it was certainly unexpected once I discovered who he was. Nevertheless, it had been so long since another man thought of my needs before his own. I had almost forgotten how sweet it felt to be taken care of.

I allowed a dripping footman to assist me from the carriage, his umbrella doing little to shield me from the bitter rain. Wincing as my stockinged feet picked their way across the gravel drive, I hurried up the steps to the front door before Lord Stallsbury could do his part to assist me once again. Inside, water dripped from my person and pooled on the marble foyer. The house was large, dark, and warm. Instantly I rebuked my

11

unkind thoughts on its lofty appearance, for I was sure to dry quickly and thoroughly in its warmth.

"Miss Clarke, it has been ages!" a voice squealed from the other side of the hallway. I turned at the sound of my maiden name. A young woman stepped forward and I recognized Miss Bancroft at once—or I supposed she was Mrs. Haley now.

"I am so glad to finally be here," I said. "The storm was worse than we expected when we first set out."

She halted just before reaching to embrace me, her hands paused midair. She did not resemble her brother at all with her dark brown hair and round cheeks. "Yes, I can see that. I shall have a bath prepared at once." She peeked around me. "And the rest of your party?"

I glanced over my shoulder. Another footman had procured an umbrella and a man was leading Emma away, doing his best to protect her from the rain.

"My carriage had trouble," I explained. "Yet we were fortunate to encounter Lord Stallsbury and Mr. Peterson on the road. They conveyed my maid and me here, but I am afraid my coachman remained behind to be with the horses." I had a sudden thought and I spun toward the approaching gentleman, ignoring the gleam in Mrs. Haley's eye. "Did my coachman happen to send my trunk?"

Lord Stallsbury had the grace to look bashful. "I am afraid we did not think of it."

Terrific. No shoes, no night clothes, no dry dress for tomorrow. Now I stood dripping water in the entranceway with nothing to change into.

"I have nothing, then," I said quietly.

"I am sure we can find you something," Mrs. Haley said cheerfully, and I did my best not to eye her short stature too closely. She turned, speaking to the man behind me. "Grant, send for a bath for Miss Clarke and see that Hannah is sent to my room."

He was off at once and she added, "Come, we will get this sorted."

"Thank you, Mrs. Haley. Though I should remind you that I am no longer Miss Clarke." And perhaps it would be incumbent of me to add that I was a good deal taller than herself.

"Oh?" she asked, beginning up the stairs.

"Yes. I am now Mrs. Wheeler." As I had been for nearly four years.

She paused, glancing at me over her shoulder. "I had forgotten. Forgive me, Mrs. Wheeler. I will do better in the future."

"It is no matter." If I had my way, I would only claim the name a few months longer anyway. We passed a large portrait hall with numerous large paintings of Bancroft men. All of them shared similar sandy-colored, curly hair and square jaws. I paused and looked up at one painting, the gentleman's expression particularly engaging. Was that what my future held? Curly-haired, square-jawed children?

A blush warmed my cheeks at the presumptuous thought. *Do not get ahead of yourself.* I still had yet to see the man. It had been years, after all, since our last encounter during the London Season.

And quite a lot could change in a person in any small amount of time. Of this, I knew firsthand.

The morning light greeted me early and I arose, dressing in a borrowed gown of coral and green that did nothing for my pale complexion and was a good three inches too short. Emma did her best to pin a length of fabric to the hem, though it was of a dismal cream and did not match in the least, forcing it to stand out excessively. It covered the snug borrowed slippers well enough, however, and was far better than showing too much ankle at my first meeting with my potential mother-in-law. I could only hope to be understandingly received when the party learned of my misfortune.

Washed out and tired from the eventful journey, in a gown that was not my own and hardly fit was not how I wished to greet my future husband, but it mattered little. There was nothing for it; I had to go down to breakfast.

Laughter trailed down the hall, traveling down my spine like an uncomfortable finger. I used to be entertaining in crowds, easily making conversation and procuring my own stream of ready laughter. Now, it seemed my life had become too deliberate for such frivolity. It was not so easy to lie about in relative carelessness when so much rested on my ability to be successful.

The closer my steps took me to the breakfast room, the higher my anxiety rose. Mr. Bancroft was not expecting a time-worn widow to step through the door, not when he had known the fanciful lady from before. Would he be disgusted by my alteration?

I stood at the door, listening to the pleasant conversation taking place on the other side.

"Are you going in?" a deep voice asked behind me.

Jumping, I clutched my heart. I caught Lord Stallsbury's gaze over my shoulder. "Eventually, I suppose."

He waited a moment, sighing. "You've obtained a gown."

"Yes." I turned to face him, poking my foot out from beneath the makeshift hem. "And slippers so tight I very well might lose the feeling in my feet. Though I suppose there are plenty of gentlemen nearby should I fall." Laughing, I sought his gaze for the shared joke. Surely if we saw amusement in the carriage ordeal it would not be uncomfortable between us. The man had *carried* me; I could still feel the warmth from where his hands had been.

He glanced at me curiously. Perhaps he did not follow my

joke. "You are lingering intentionally, Mrs. Wheeler. Have you just cause for such an action?"

I said nothing. I'd been caught out. And Lord Stallsbury, it seemed, did not find humor easily in the mornings.

He brushed past me, opening the door and waiting for me to walk through it, impatience clear in the set of his mouth.

He'd forced my hand. I had no other recourse but to walk into the room. Whether I appreciated this or was repelled by it, I could not tell. What I did know was I had no choice, and I quickly stepped through the door and into a room of utter silence.

If only the occupants were still laughing, then at least I would have avoided the unwelcome stares found on every face in the room.

I swallowed. That was untrue and I knew it. I was not unwelcome. I had come to Bancroft Hill by express invitation to court a man. It was only natural that everyone at the house party would be aware of the situation. Gossip did not sit still for very long. They likely only stared because they were curious.

"Good morning," I said to the room at large, delivering a curtsy on shaky legs.

Chair legs scraped against the floor as Mr. Bancroft stood with haste, setting his napkin carefully on the table. Our eyes locked across the room as though we were the only two occupants.

He looked very much the same. Curly, sandy blonde hair, tousled in a state of perfected disarray, brown eyes, and a steady brow. He was as constant and stable as a trusty hound dog, and equally as gentle. The intensity of his gaze said he was perhaps *not* disappointed by the changes he saw in me—for surely there were many.

"Mrs. Wheeler," he said, bowing before me. "I heard of your unfortunate experience yesterday. I apologize for the horrid condition in which you found the roads."

I laughed with gentle ease, much to my own surprise. "You can hardly be faulted for the state of the roads, Mr. Bancroft. Though I appreciate the sentiment all the same."

"Come, Mrs. Wheeler," Mrs. Haley said from her seat at the table, snapping me to awareness of the other eyes watching us. "You must be ravenous."

I sat in the empty chair beside Mr. Bancroft and waited as he filled a plate for me at the sideboard.

Mrs. Bancroft watched me from her seat across the table, her gaze crawling over my skin like tiny bugs.

I met my potential mother-in-law's eyes, determined to say something that would paint me in a flattering light. Her shrewd gaze pierced me, silencing my thoughts at once.

"Mrs. Wheeler," she said, "how nice it is that you chose to join us this week."

Did she truly feel so? I could not tell. Finding my voice, I replied, "I am glad to be here. It has been ages since I enjoyed a house party."

"Yes, I'd imagine so."

I leaned back to allow room for the plate Mr. Bancroft filled for me. He must have taken his sister's exclamation literally. Food mounded the plate near to overflowing.

I thanked him, using my fork to push aside sausages, kippers and pastries. With the eyes of so many strangers watching, I could not take a single bite.

A woman glided into the room, taking her seat beside an older man I didn't recognize at the other end of the table. Her gown was a delicate confection and her nose trained closer to the ceiling than the floor.

"Miss Pollard, you are looking lovely this morning," Mrs. Bancroft said, her tone dripping honey. "A night of rest has done much to restore you."

"It has, thank you."

The older gentleman beside her rose and filled a plate for her as she waited. Her gaze appraised me, a delicate line marring her brow. "William," she purred, "do introduce us. I have anticipated this moment for an age."

I took a quick bite to cover my shock. Clearly they were on close terms to use Christian names at the breakfast table, and before other guests, too. I would assume there was an understanding between them had I not been invited to Bancroft Hill for that very purpose.

I could not tell whether the swirl of unease in my stomach was due to Miss Pollard and her perfectly coiffed head or the kipper I unwittingly shoved into my mouth.

"Please allow me the honor, Miss Pollard," Mr. Bancroft said, eyeing her with deliberation. Clearly uncomfortable with the use of his Christian name, he held her gaze a moment longer before introducing us, then continuing about the room, introducing me to Mr. Pollard, the woman's stout father, who was busy retrieving her breakfast, and Mr. Peterson, who had entered the room at that moment.

"I absolutely cannot wait to get to know you, Mrs. Wheeler," Miss Pollard said, eyeing me with a small grin. She did not allow Mr. Bancroft's subtle chastisement to derail her, and for that I had to admire her. "I shall fill your head with stories of Mr. Bancroft's misdeeds and we can laugh together over his silly childhood antics."

"I should think you would assist me, Miss Pollard," Mr. Bancroft replied, "and only share those anecdotes which might be complimentary."

Miss Pollard's laugh rang clear through the room. "As though you need any help creating a good name for yourself."

Her disbelief was relatable. Mr. Bancroft was the very image of chivalrous civility. He was refined preciseness, from the clothing he wore to the perfect haphazard placement of his curls. It was a blessed miracle the man remained yet unwed.

"We have planned a great many things to occupy our time,"

Mrs. Bancroft said, stealing the attention from every member of the room. My gaze traveled the length of the table, resting upon Lord Stallsbury and Mr. Peterson where they sat at the far end in quiet conversation. They were rather reserved this morning. Perhaps that was typical behavior for them, but it did not fall in line with the stories I'd heard of the *man about town*.

"And we thought," Mr. Bancroft added, turning his slightly anxious gaze on me, "to begin with an archery tournament. Should you find that to your liking, Mrs. Wheeler?"

I pressed the toes of my borrowed slippers into the floor. Could he mean today? I was poorly outfitted and lacked proper footwear, but I would not let that get in the way of what little time we had to reacquaint ourselves. I had very little time and a large order to fill. I needed to get my hands on a pair of sturdier shoes forthwith. "That would be lovely."

He beamed at me, his cheeks tingeing pink in a most becoming way. I laughed to cover my nerves and trained my gaze back on my plate, but not before catching Lord Stallsbury's inquisitive stare just over Mr. Bancroft's shoulder.

The butterflies in my midsection beat a rapid measure. I felt the heat of Mr. Bancroft's gaze warm my neck. It appeared his affection was as unchanged as his appearance. I only hoped I would not disappoint him.

CHAPTER 3

Removing to my room to gather my bonnet and shawl, I came upon a brown paper package nestled in the doorway of my bedchamber.

"Emma," I called, bringing the parcel inside and closing the door. "What is this?"

She glanced up from the bedclothes she'd been fixing. "I don't know, miss."

Peeling back the thick paper to reveal brown leather, I gasped. "Emma, someone has gotten me shoes! I can hardly credit it. However would they have done so with such speed?"

She shrugged, clearly not as enthralled with the mystery as I. I would have thought the idea of a mystery would entice her. It was certainly captivating to me.

"But who could have done so?" Fingering the supple leather, I sat on the edge of my bed and removed the slippers from my feet. Mrs. Haley was shorter than me and in possession of smaller feet, and I was at once relieved to stretch my toes. Pulling on the well-made half-boots, I sighed. They were a touch too large, but otherwise a perfectly comfortable fit.

Mr. Bancroft had mentioned just that morning at breakfast

how he was sorry to hear about my ordeal, so he must have been informed about my missing shoes as well and sent a servant directly to obtain me a new pair. There was no other reasonable explanation. Lord Stallsbury and Mr. Peterson both were present and aware of the mud stealing my shoes, but surely neither of them would gift me such a large and costly item.

My heart swelled as Emma knelt down and laced the boots. I jumped up, took a few turns about the room and halted near the window. It overlooked the estate and duck pond, as well as a grove of trees on the far side. Bancroft Hill was grander than any home I'd lived in, and Mr. Bancroft was a kind and chivalrous gentleman. True, nothing was certain, but for a moment I allowed myself to give into the hope swelling in my heart. I could be happy at Bancroft Hill. I was sure of it.

There was a fine stable on the opposite side of the house, and it contained, I was sure, an array of suitable mares for Charlotte to ride. She was positively horse mad and I could easily picture her galloping about the estate after I wed Mr. Bancroft and brought her to live with me. She would be happy here, too.

The sun, peeking through soft clouds, lit the rolling lawn and filtered through my window, warming me. I had made the correct decision in coming to Bancroft Hill. I would not let this opportunity pass.

"Have you participated in archery before?" Miss Pollard asked, strolling beside me across the immaculately cut lawn. Her soft pink gown and matching ribbon sewn through her hair were lovely, frilly confections that seemed more suited to a drawing room than a damp lawn. The storm from yesterday had receded, much like Mr. Peterson predicted, yet the chill and cloudy sky remained a steady reminder that the weather could turn around quickly if it pleased.

"Not in quite a few years," I answered. My marriage had not been privileged enough to claim an estate with its own lawn. It had been years since I'd lived in a house with enough space for the sport. I had not participated in lawn games since my youth.

"That will probably run in your favor," she said, coming closer and lowering her voice. "The men appreciate a win. Do not endeavor to put yourself out."

"Is that a universal fact?" I asked.

She nodded, sure of herself. "Of course."

The only man currently in my life was my brother, Noah, and he was not usually alert enough to play any games, let alone care who won or lost. And my marriage was too much of a sham to really give me any true credence on what men did or did not appreciate.

"Thank you for the insight."

She smiled, lifting her chin. "Of course. We women ought to stick together."

I was usually a sound judge of character, but I had yet to make out Miss Pollard's. Her familiarity with Mr. Bancroft set off a warning within me, but her casual glances at the other men in the party had not gone unnoticed, either.

We arrived at the targets after the men, who stood around the table investigating the arrows. I watched them each for any sign that they would notice my footwear, or toss a casual glance at my feet, but was sorely disappointed when none of them seemed inclined to notice that I had donned new half-boots. Discovering the anonymous benefactor was more difficult than I had anticipated.

"Where is Mrs. Haley?" I asked, after greeting Mr. Bancroft.

"She does not care for sporting," he replied. "Unless we entice her with a picnic, I am afraid she will find a better use of her time."

I picked up an arrow from the table and ran it lightly through my fingers. "Then we simply must plan a picnic." I placed the arrow back on the table, glancing toward the house. "Is her husband present? I did not meet him at breakfast."

He smiled endearingly, his head tilting slightly to the side. "Mr. Haley was far too busy in London to come for the entire party. He shall arrive at the end for the ball, but he could not be spared at present, or so he claimed. He is an aspiring politician, you know." He reached forward and lifted a long, sleek bow. "Now, are you familiar with archery?"

"A little rusty, but I can manage." I tried to deliver an encouraging smile. I must have been successful if his answering grin was any clue.

Miss Pollard and I were armed with bows, docking our arrows side by side.

"Each of us shall take a turn," Mr. Bancroft explained, "and the farthest arrow from the center will be eliminated at the end of each round. We will repeat the process until we have crowned a winner."

"And what shall the winner receive?" Mr. Peterson asked with a smug grin.

Mr. Bancroft said, "Prestige, of course."

Miss Pollard giggled and I would have liked to shut my ears to the grating sound. It was clearly exaggerated. She turned to me and said, "You may begin," as though she was doing me the grandest favor.

I had once enjoyed this sport immensely and the feel of the arrow between my fingers reminded me of peaceful days past. I weighed the importance of Miss Pollard's words as I gauged the distance of the target with its painted black and blue circles. Certainly I was overthinking the process, but it had been so long and I keenly felt the gazes of all the spectators upon me.

The arrow slipped from my fingers before I was prepared to

send it on its way and it flew at an angle before plopping onto the grass halfway between me and the target. Drat.

Polite clapping punctuated my irritation. Oh well, perhaps it was for the best. Hadn't Miss Pollard said the men enjoyed winning?

Pulling her elbow back, Miss Pollard's arrow flew steady, plunking into the painted target across the lawn, near the center.

So much for going easy on the men, then, I supposed.

Mr. Bancroft gave me a commiserating smile before taking his place next, beside Mr. Peterson. Both of them sank their arrows near Miss Pollard's.

I stepped back, clasping my hands and doing my utmost to swallow my frustration. I had looked inept, with no opportunity to redeem myself in this round. Unless Lord Stallsbury's arrow fell further from the target than mine, I would be out of the competition.

He sidled up beside me. "Your arrow has gone missing, Mrs. Wheeler."

My gaze sweeping the grass, it took a moment to see the dark wood laying just between us and the painted targets. I pointed. "It is just there."

"Ah." He nodded. "I see that you are a proficient."

His playful tone belied the unkind words and I smiled in spite of myself. "I *was* at one point. But all talents fade in time, I suppose."

"When they are left unpracticed, surely." His eyebrows lifted. "Were you once a master of archery?"

"There was a time when I would have likely hit the center of the target." My cheeks warmed and I turned to him. "Forgive my boastfulness. It has been ages since I've held a bow and the arrow slipped from my fingers. I am merely vexed that I lost the opportunity to at least hit the board."

"I see."

I smiled wryly, watching Mr. Bancroft laugh with Mr. Peterson over the nearness of their arrows. "An amateur mistake, to be sure."

He tipped his head. "Then we must allow you to redeem yourself."

Had he not heard the rules of the competition? I could not redeem myself until the competition was over. Though perhaps that is what he meant.

He stepped to the white chalked line and docked an arrow, glancing at me so briefly that I could very well have imagined it.

The spectators quieted as though his very concentration demanded respect, eagerly watching Lord Stallsbury's reserved concentration. He pulled his elbow back squarely before suddenly turning it down and letting it go. The arrow released and stuck in the ground not three paces from where he stood.

Mr. Bancroft laughed, clapping his hands. "Capital, Stallsbury! Superbly gracious, to be sure. Why did I not think of it myself?"

All eyes turned on me and I felt my cheeks flush. The chivalry was much appreciated, yet a fire within me would not allow the sacrifice to go unchallenged. My stubborn pride reared its ugly head. Had Lord Stallsbury merely wished to see me sink an arrow into the center of the target? I was fairly certain I plainly explained to him that my talent was practiced long ago.

Lord Stallsbury handed me the bow, his grin unrelenting.

"Thank you, sir. I appreciate the sacrifice."

He bowed slightly. "I am sure it will be worth it."

I watched him move to stand beside the other men, my heart beating rapidly as their eyes all trained on me. Nerves that were previously absent skittered about my chest. I had boasted I could hit the target; I had no choice now but to deliver.

Docking my arrow, I pulled my elbow back, focusing on the blue circle at the center of the target much like Noah had taught me to do when we were younger. The arrow felt slick in my sweaty fingers, tapping against my wrist guard, and I directed it before it could slide free on its own accord once again.

I released it, gratified at the thunk of the arrow hitting wood. It landed outside the largest circle on the target, but it had made it. Of that, I was infinitely relieved.

"Well done, Mrs. Wheeler," Mr. Bancroft shouted, his face a picture of pride as though I had sunk one in the very center of the target.

I turned and offered a curtsy, taken aback by Lord Stallsbury's smug smile. The cad! I had never expressly said I could hit the center today; only that I had in the past. I longed to pick up another arrow and practice until I was proficient again when a fat drop of water fell onto my nose.

"Rain!" Miss Pollard shrieked, dropping her bow immediately.

Mr. Bancroft removed his large coat at once, holding it over Miss Pollard as they made a dash for the house.

I did not know whether to praise his regard for a woman's care or feel slighted that he had not exhibited the same care for me.

The weather was nothing compared to the drenching I'd received yesterday. I turned for the house, crossing my arms around my stomach as the remaining two men flanked me.

Mr. Peterson eyed me seriously. "I should think you are a cursed woman, Mrs. Wheeler."

He did not know the half of it. I smiled politely, his grin making up for the remark. "You blame me for the weather, Mr. Peterson?"

"Have you any defense? I've yet to see you outside when we have not been visited with rain."

I laughed, despite the ridiculous flirtation. "Our acquaintance is two days old, sir. I should think that we may declare this a coincidence at present."

"Of course, madam," he said gravely. "But remind me to

bring an umbrella the next time we venture out of doors together."

I shot him a wry smile, which he returned. Lord Stallsbury was unamused, his gaze trained on Mr. Bancroft and Miss Pollard ahead of us.

"You've known Bancroft long, then?" Mr. Peterson inquired, turning the nature of the conversation.

"We met in London during the Season nearly five years ago," I explained. "I had to leave abruptly due to the death of my parents, and we lost connection at that point." In truth, I had reached out to Mr. Bancroft after being shipped away to my aunt's house, but never received a reply to my letter. Though I had not been eager to accept his hand right away, I would have done so during my mourning if only to escape the stifling, oppressive home of my aunt.

Lord Stallsbury opened the front door for me. His dampened hair fell over his furrowed brow, his brown eyes as stormy as the sky.

"Sir?" I asked. He had seemed quite pleasant before. The change was as swift as it was unprecedented.

"Andrew," he said over the top of my head. "Meet me in the library. I've something to discuss with you."

Mr. Peterson laughed, shaking his head as though he antici-pated this. I was beginning to see that such merriment was a common occurrence for the man. "That sounds ominous."

"It is nothing of the sort."

Lord Stallsbury bowed to me, spinning on his heel and mounting the steps toward the bedchambers with great speed. I watched him go as the butler approached.

"Send my man up," Mr. Peterson demanded before dipping his head toward me. "I shall see you later this evening, Mrs. Wheeler."

Left alone with the butler, I turned expectant eyes on him. "Yes?"

"Your carriage has been retrieved and the grooms are seeing to your broken wheel at present."

Relief poured through me. If it was an easy fix then surely Mr. Bancroft would not require payment. "My trunk?" I inquired.

"It has been delivered to your room."

Breath left me in a rush. They were dowdy compared to Miss Pollard's fashionable frocks, but I was glad to have my own gowns nonetheless.

Wind howled past the windows as rain pattered lightly against the panes. The rain did not appear the least inclined to let up. I huffed. Perhaps Mr. Peterson had been correct. There was a chance that I was, indeed, cursed.

CHAPTER 4

Sleep eluded me. Though on the smaller side, the bedchamber was cozy. Large, thick drapes encircled the bed and kept in the warmth, and I did not lack for either candles or my gothic reading material.

Sighing, I dropped my head back and closed the book on my lap.

I had read enough of my novel to learn that the scarred highwayman was, indeed, likely to end up the hero, and found that despite the romanticism, I simply could not stomach completing the story at present. I tucked the book back into my trunk, shoving it under my spare chemise and layering my lavender spencer over the top of it.

It was not lost on me that the fictional highwayman laid claim to dark hair and a brooding temperament, much like the man who had saved me on the highway in the rain. Lord Stallsbury's pensive nature of late was nothing like the man I had heard gossiped about in recent years.

A young, eligible, sought-after gentleman with a penchant for adventure and a taste for danger, Lord Stallsbury had been discussed for his string of potential wives and subsequent duels.

With such a reputation, it was shocking that he had yet to flirt very much of his own accord. Though his easy amusement was quite evident in moments, his temperament did not quite line up with the person I had heard rumors about during my Season.

I rubbed my eyes. Whatever was the matter with me? Whether Lord Stallsbury had a reputation or not mattered little. I was here for one man, and one reason only. To become engaged.

How else would I save my sister?

That was it. *Lottie.* Surely she was the reason I was incapable of sleep. I had yet to receive word that she was being taken care of, that she was comfortable. I believed Miss Hurst would provide a safe home for Charlotte, but I still worried, however illogical that worry might be.

Perhaps if I wrote to Charlotte, I would be able to fall asleep. Surely at this time of night, I could complete my task and return to bed with no one the wiser.

I gathered my dressing gown about me, tying the sash snugly around my waist. Carrying the candle, I snuck from my room, down the darkened hallway and to the staircase. When I married Frank, I'd had many lonely, sleepless nights. He was gone almost directly following our wedding. The wife of an army captain during a war leads a solitary existence—one that I was glad to be done with.

Standing in the hallway downstairs, I could not recall which of the doors belonged to the library. Mrs. Haley had pointed out the correct one earlier that day in the event that I found myself in need of a book or some paper. I stepped forward, placing my hand against the door to my right. The floorboard creaked beneath my foot, startling me, and I jumped back. No, could it be the other door? I turned around, letting myself inside the opposite, identical doorway. Though the room was dark, a man's touch was still evident in the heavy wooden bookcases lining the wall beside the door.

I'd found it. I stepped forward, holding my candle close to read the titles.

Boring things, the lot of them. Agriculture guides and history, a book about farming which was particularly thick. Whatever could be so intensive about farming to require such a thick manual? I set down the candle on a nearby ledge and pulled the large volume from the shelf, flipping through dry pages in slight disgust. Surely the house had novels, as well. Whatever did they spend their free time reading? Irrigation systems?

"Just choosing a bit of light reading for the middle of the night?"

I jumped, dropping the book on my foot. I cried out, spinning around to search the dark for the owner of the voice, though I knew with an odd innateness to whom it belonged.

"Lord Stallsbury," I admonished, "whatever are you thinking, frightening me so?"

"Are you hurt?" he questioned, materializing from the shadows. His coat removed and sleeves rolled up, I should have had the grace to look away. Marriage, however, and living with my brother had allowed me to grow used to the sight of a man in his shirtsleeves, and it did not bother me as it once would have.

Though the sight of *Lord Stallsbury* in his shirtsleeves elicited an entirely different response than my brother, or even Frank ever had.

The top of my foot throbbed something fierce and I limped to the large wingback chair closest to me, falling into it with unladylike inelegance. He came around with swift agility, seating himself in the chair beside mine. His dark eyebrows were pulled together, shadows from the lone candle upon the bookcase behind us marking creased concern on his face.

"It is nothing," I reassured him, longing to pull my foot from its stocking and check the depth of the bruise that was surely growing.

"I glanced through that book earlier today," he said, indicating the one I had just dropped. "I can quite comfortably say that it was a great deal heavier than *nothing*."

"You've an interest in agriculture, my lord?"

His eyes tightened, though that could be owed to the darkness of the room. "I am simply doing proper research, as any landowner ought to do."

The pulsating throb in my foot was quieting now, though remained sufficient to keep my attention from straying too far from it. "I thought being a landowner simply required a dutiful and knowledgeable land steward, but perhaps I am simply old fashioned. Where is your land situated, if you don't mind my prying?"

"Northumberland," he said, his brow a mixture of confusion and bewilderment. "My brother used to bemoan his ability to throw a stone from our rooftop that could easily hit Scotland. Though that was untrue, it is quite close."

"Quite north, indeed, then."

"Have you visited?"

I looked away. Would he know of my deceit were I to attempt it? "Yes," I answered, surprising myself. His deep brown eyes called to me of home in a way that I could not quite decipher. It was unnatural that I would feel such a connection to a man I hardly knew, but I felt the desire to trust him.

He studied my face, his gaze falling toward my feet a time or two. That must be it, he was merely attempting to distract me from my pain.

"I have an aunt in Northumberland, actually," I continued. "I stayed with her for half a year before my marriage. It was a beautiful land, and I think I quite miss the cows above all else."

His head jerked toward me. "Cows? Wretched creatures."

I laughed. "How dare you impugn such glorious beasts. They are the providers of cheese, you must know. And a great deal of things are made significantly better due to cheese."

"Yes, like what exactly?"

I met his challenging gaze and held it. "Toasted cheese, for one."

Clearly he had not expected that answer.

I settled further into my chair, recalling times my father would make us toasted cheese beside the fire. "Without the cheese, it would simply be toasted bread. I find myself craving it when the storms rage and the fires bellow. There is nothing that tastes quite like home as toasted cheese."

The window rattled with wind and rain as if on demand. "Then I shall endeavor to produce some for you."

I laughed. "Good heavens, sir. I could not possibly eat *now*. I fairly gorged myself at dinner."

A smile touched his lips. "You speak so plainly. You are aware of this, I assume."

"I have been told a time or two that my opinions are quite determined, yes," I answered.

Though, to be fair, I had not heard the complaint in quite some time. Not since before the passing of my parents four years prior. I could hardly credit it at present.

His voice was quiet, his words measured. "Then perhaps you could assist me in solving a riddle."

I pulled my thick dressing gown tighter around myself. "That would depend upon the nature of the riddle, my lord. If it is agriculture to which you refer then I'm afraid I am quite inept."

He chuckled, the sound traveling up my spine in a not wholly unpleasant manner. He ran a hand over his shadowed face. "There is a man—a close friend of mine—who is in a great dilemma. He has been informed that unless he correctly alters his attitude—by marriage, no less—he shall be cut off completely."

"That is a grave dilemma, indeed."

He glanced away, his eyes searching the darkness. "His father is robust. It will likely be years before he inherits, and in the interim he would, essentially, be penniless. Though, that is not the dilemma," he continued. "The issue he faces is that he would quite prefer to be cut off."

I had not expected that. "And your friend truly means this? Clearly he's never struggled to put food upon his table. There are many who would wish for wealth, even if marriage were the qualifying factor. A large part of England would wish it, I should think."

His face looked at me sharply. "Why, though? What is the appeal?"

Was he mad? Surely he must be mad. Only a man who grew up with immense fortune would not understand the appeal, for he had never had to live with the loss.

He stood, walking into the dark side of the room and then back toward me.

"Lord Stallsbury," I said softly. "Shall we drop the pretenses?"

He dropped into his chair once again as though in agreeance, so I sallied forth.

"I am sure you realize I am not a young miss and subsequently, that I am quite clever. I am assuming the friend of which you speak is, in fact, yourself. If I am being presumptuous, then do please stop me at any moment."

I paused, locked on his uncertain gaze. When he said nothing, I continued. "It seems to me that you haven't a riddle to be solved as much as you have a decision to make. Whichever path you choose, you must do so with utmost certainty, for that is how you will confidently face your trials. And regardless of the path you take, there will undoubtedly be many trials."

"A pretty speech. And better advice in one breath than I received this afternoon over the course of an hour."

I chuckled, for he must have been referring to his interview with Mr. Peterson. He had requested the man's company, had he not? "I have learned through my own mistakes that a lack of certainty will lead to far too much self-pity and unnecessary pain."

"Though how can you be certain you have made the correct choice?"

I lifted one shoulder in a tired shrug. "You cannot. That is where you must have faith in the logic you follow." As I did not, when I hastily married the first man who showed me any sort of affection. I had not realized at the time that his was fleeting.

Lord Stallsbury's gaze took on a contemplative element and I rose, wincing at the pain in my foot as I stepped away.

"Allow me to escort you upstairs," he offered.

I smiled at him, tilting my head. "Come now, my lord. It is wrong enough that we are alone in this room. If we were to be discovered near our bedrooms it would be detrimental."

"True. I should not like to make an enemy of Bancroft," he replied, amusement glittering in his eyes.

I delivered a wry smile. "He is likely the kindest man I know. I would not fear him if I were you."

"I was referring to his mother."

I laughed, louder than I meant to. The prim woman was a force to behold, that was certain. I curtsied. "Goodnight, my lord."

"Goodnight, Mrs. Wheeler."

Floating back up to my room with the single candle guiding my way, I left him in the same darkness in which I had found him earlier. I only hoped that the shadows did not extend to the man's heart, as well.

CHAPTER 5

The unfortunate thing about house parties was that regardless of who was in attendance, one had no other choice but to remain in their presence for the duration. Miss Pollard had so far proved that she was just the sort of female who would delight in being rescued by a scarred highwayman who turned out to be a wealthy earl, or some such fictional fantasy like the heroine in my book. She was exactly the sort of silly female who forced me to use great restraint.

I should have known the moment she fled the archery tournament due to a sprinkling of rain that she was given to hysterics. What I was unprepared for was her deep, abiding fear of ducks.

"It is *coming* toward me!" she whined, leaping behind me.

It was comforting to know that she valued her safety above my own. "I believe they are waddling that direction," I said, pointing toward the pond.

Her hands gripped my shoulders, peeking around me. "You are certain?"

"Of course she is not certain," Mrs. Haley said, watching us with some bafflement. "Who can predict the intentions of a duck?"

"Exactly," Miss Pollard said with conviction.

The ducks did indeed waddle to the pond, let themselves into the water and swam in the shallows. I stepped away from Miss Pollard's grip. "Shall we resume our walk?"

"I would prefer to move away from the pond if we can help it."

"Of course, dear," Mrs. Haley said, drawing Miss Pollard's arm around her own and setting off across the lawn. She shot me a look before saying kindly, "Shall we return home? I am utterly spent."

I fell into step alongside them. "The wood is lovely," I hinted. "Have you any wild animals lurking within?"

"Not to my knowledge."

I listened to the women discuss the ball that was to complete the house party. Miss Pollard had brought with her three gowns for the occasion and could not choose which she would wear. It was a blessing indeed that we had more than a fortnight to help her make her choice.

Three horses appeared in the distance, their course altering in our direction. Lord Stallsbury's eyes were bright, but the shadows from last night were still evident in the creases beside his eyes and the firm set to his lips.

He sat upon a fine horse which would have caused Charlotte to swoon. I could not help but watch the gentle gait of the superior creature, imagining my sister on such a beast. Oh, how she would grin. When I married, she would be able to have all that she deserved.

"Good day, ladies. It is a fine day for a walk," Mr. Bancroft said, swinging from his horse and landing on the ground in a graceful thud.

"Any day is made finer on these beautiful grounds," Miss

Pollard simpered, her voice turning high and airy in the presence of the men.

I glanced above me; surely they were joking. The thick, gray clouds hadn't ceased to cover the sun in ages. While we had enough light to consider a walk outdoors and the clouds were far from ominous, they could turn into the pouring rain we'd been experiencing in a matter of moments. Surely Mr. Bancroft and Miss Pollard were aware that it was not, in fact, a *fine* day. It *might* be called a decent one, comparatively speaking, but fine was definitely an exaggeration.

"Mrs. Wheeler, I would very much like to know what you think of it?" Lord Stallsbury inquired, pulling his horse about to face us.

I had been singled out. And judging by the amusement on his lips, he was aware of my inattention. "Of what in particular are you referring, my lord?"

"The ball."

Had they been speaking of the ball again? I wouldn't know.

"Your face was carrying quite an array of emotions," he continued. "I anxiously await your opinions."

"As do I," Mr. Bancroft added magnanimously. "I have always valued your ideals."

Always? We had known each other during the Season, but it was not a lengthy acquaintance. Two months, at best. I straightened my shawl, pulling the soft material higher about my shoulders to ward off the chilling wind. "Forgive me then, for I was not attending the conversation."

Miss Pollard laughed cheerfully. "I was only saying that I should be delighted if we were to visit the moddiste in town. I am sure we have all brought proper ball gowns, of course, but a nice ribbon or new set of gloves may be just the thing to celebrate our enjoyable visit here at Bancroft Hill."

Essentially, then, Miss Pollard desired an excuse to shop. Far be it from me to stand in her way. "I should love an outing to the village. I was unable to see much on our journey in."

Lord Stallsbury smiled the grin of a cat on the hunt. "And do you think we shall make an outing of it?"

Thunder sounded in the distance and our heads all turned in unison. Drat. Maybe Mr. Peterson was right.

"Shall we proceed to the house?" Mrs. Haley inquired, a nervous looking Miss Pollard clutching her arm.

"Indeed," I responded.

Mr. Bancroft jumped from his horse and offered his elbow. "May I escort you?"

Nodding, I slipped my hand around his arm. He led me at a slower pace than that of his sister and Miss Pollard. The men had dipped their hats and rode toward the stables, leaving Mr. Bancroft and I to walk back to the house in relative privacy, our only companion his horse trailing dutifully behind.

"How have you kept yourself busy these last few years?" he inquired.

Did he prefer the long answer or the polite one? "You know I was married."

"Yes, an army captain, wasn't it? He died at Waterloo?"

I nodded. "That was it, yes."

Bancroft watched me and I found I could not return his gaze. "You poor woman, to be widowed so young, and so soon after your marriage."

"I am not alone in my circumstance. Many women were thus widowed. We lived in a time of war, sir."

"Glad I am that we are out of it."

The effects of the war still raged in homes across England, but I was glad we were not fighting any longer. With my husband, or other countries.

"But he was a good man?"

I halted, my body growing tense. I had thought he was, when

we married. It was thanks to the war that I was never forced to realize the extent of Frank's temper. I shuddered.

"You are cold. Come, let us make haste into the house."

Gray clouds rolled in with slow satisfaction, thunder rumbling behind us as if the weather was laughing at our plight.

"Is this not meant to be summer?" Bancroft asked with irritation. "I'd chosen these weeks to feature Bancroft Hill's exquisite countryside and beautiful valleys. You shall not even have a chance to enjoy the outdoors if this wretched weather persists."

He could not control the weather. Rain was simply a part of life. Particularly that of British life. "The weather matters little when surrounded by such excellent company."

"You flatter me, my dear," he said, his grin belying the staid response.

If only his words flattered me, as well. I had yet to feel the butterflies of attraction I'd once experienced before marrying Frank. Still, there was something to be said for his consistency of character. I had learned from personal experience that the man you face at the altar on your wedding day can easily change into a different person following the vows. It was encouraging that the years had done nothing to alter Mr. Bancroft. I had a feeling that marriage would do nothing to his personality either.

CHAPTER 6

The blue silk gown was a particular favorite of mine. I had put extensive effort into embroidering Forget-Me-Nots into the hem and neckline. Wide white ribbon lined the seam under the bust and tied in the back, trailing down the gown. I liked to think it was elegant in its simplicity. I floated down the staircase, my head high under Emma's superior skill with the curling tongs, confidence flowing through me.

My spirit deflated the moment I stepped through the door. The other women in the party instantly outshone me in the drawing room before dinner. I did my best not to find excessive fault with my gown after facing the superior workmanship and style that graced the other ladies; their gowns were clearly made to fit the latest trends.

Lord Stallsbury looked up from his place near the mantle, catching my eye with an appraising look of his own. I hovered near the door, unsure, before moving toward him, the other women in the room deep in conversation.

"Mr. Pollard does not know how to remain upright without assistance," he said as I approached.

I stifled my laugh, purposefully avoiding the wide man whose snore reverberated from his chest and through the room.

"He must have been here long before anyone else," I guessed.

"Wrong," Lord Stallsbury said. "He entered shortly before you did."

Mr. Pollard's snore was particularly jarring in that moment, though it did not seem to bother his daughter whatsoever, who sat in conversation with Mrs. Bancroft and Mrs. Haley nearby. She must be quite used to the sound, it would seem.

Dinner was announced and Mr. Bancroft approached me, bowing over my hand. "You look enchanting, Mrs. Wheeler."

"Thank you," I said, dipping a curtsy.

He grinned, his face lighting up. He led me into the dining room, seating me on his right as the guest of honor. If any member of the party had previously doubted Mr. Bancroft's intentions, those doubts were surely put to rest by his actions.

Mrs. Bancroft sat at the foot of the table, and I felt her beady eyes upon me through the duration of the meal. She had not liked me much in London when we had met years prior during the Season, and I clearly had not grown in her esteem in the interim.

I spent dinner listening to Mr. Bancroft explain his favorite aspects of the house and parish. There seemed to be much to see in the small town nearby and quite a few places in the house in which I had yet to explore.

His few stories from childhood often included Miss Pollard, and it was clear that she was his childhood playmate and dear friend of the family.

"The library is stunning," he said, "with an extensive collection of books quite unlike anything you've previously seen, I am sure. It is unrivaled in the county, for my father was well known for his affinity for reading and collecting books of various types and sizes."

My thoughts instantly traveled to my foot. Yes, I had experienced the *large size* of one of Mr. Bancroft's books myself. Though the size of the library was lost on me as I'd only had an opportunity to see it in the dark, my single candle insufficient light for proper exploration. Thinking on that night brought Lord Stallsbury and his very personal dilemma to mind, but I pushed the thoughts aside. It would do me no good to give the man any extra consideration. He came unbidden into my thoughts often enough as it was.

"I should love to give you a tour of the library tomorrow," Mr. Bancroft said.

I dipped my head. "That would be lovely, sir. I am, myself, quite an avid reader."

Lord Stallsbury asked, "And what is it you enjoy reading, Mrs. Wheeler?"

I caught his amused gaze and hoped my pale face confirmed placid interest. "Novels, mostly."

"You do not enjoy light reading about topics of interest?" he continued, picking up his glass and languidly swirling his wine. "Farming, perhaps? Or irrigation studies?"

Mr. Bancroft coughed, covering his mouth with his napkin to avoid spraying the table with food. "Gads, sir. What purpose would Mrs. Wheeler have reading about farming?"

"None, I suppose," Lord Stallsbury replied, sipping his wine. He shot me a wink so subtle that I imagined I fabricated it. "I only wondered if her extensive reading expanded beyond novels. Interesting things, to be sure, but quite spoiling for a young woman when consumed in excess, I believe."

My spine stiffened. I lowered my fork so as not to use it accidentally as a weapon. Novels had been my escape for quite a few years. Through the duration of my stay with my aunt, my marriage and the subsequent loneliness in each of those situations, I read to pretend I was elsewhere. After I had taken charge over Lottie and we were forced to move in with our brother, I read even more. All of these things were circumstances that I had little control over, but not situations in which I had to remain. My novels did much to allow me to travel to other times and places the likes of which I would never know firsthand. I had married a man who held less regard for me than he did his prized hound, a mistake I vowed to never make again. Yet, through all of the heartache, I had survived because I had imaginary worlds to escape to.

"I am no bluestocking, my lord," I said eventually, defending myself. "And I have long found novels to be an unexceptional form of entertainment for a young woman."

"Hear, hear!" Mr. Bancroft applauded. "I should think you'd support reading novels, Stallsbury. Your own brother writes them."

"I have yet to read Cameron's books," he replied, his eyes turning dark. "Though I am fond of his wife, and I am sure they write lovely books, I find my taste runs in quite another direction."

I attempted to look as guileless as possible. "Farming and irrigation studies, my lord?"

His lips fought a grin, and my heart beat furiously as he said, "Naturally. Useful topics, to be sure."

Returning my attention to my dish, I felt the faint bruise on my foot call to me. It was a phantom pain of a bruise undisturbed. But the pleasant, forbidden interaction of last evening in the library left a warmth in my heart that I did not comprehend.

"Might I persuade you to entertain us this evening, Mrs. Wheeler?" Mr. Bancroft asked, pulling my attention from my own musings. It was hard not to sit taller when his eager gaze rested on me. "Your voice is quite unforgettable, though I should enjoy the reminder."

I dipped my head in acquiescence. "I would be delighted."

He grinned, and I glanced at Lord Stallsbury before I thought better of it. He watched me unabashedly, the smile on his lips teasing me while his shadowed eyes revealed a deeper meaning to his playful banter. Though of a nature I could not understand, the dilemma he laid out for me in the library was nothing to smirk at. I did not envy the decision he had to make, nor did I understand the depth to it. Though I could suppose, given his reputation within Society, that it was a tool his parents were using to attempt to force him to settle down. If only I saw the rake within him to back up the rumors, for now I could not fathom the connection between the man I heard stories of and the one sitting across the table from me.

Miss Pollard on Lord Stallsbury's opposite side called his attention and I watched them interact, his lighthearted pleasantry giving no hint of his deeper dilemma.

When the women were excused after dinner, I followed my hostess into the drawing room, installing myself on the bench of the pianoforte right away. Mrs. Bancroft did not seem disturbed in the least by my removal from the women. She made herself busy with quiet conversation on the sofa, Mrs. Haley and Miss Pollard dutifully holding court.

Sifting through the available sheet music, I chose a piece I hadn't played in some time but once knew well, warming up my fingers on the ivory keys. I was aware of the women's eyes warming my back as they spoke. I was undoubtedly the topic of their conversation, though I tried not to let the fact bother me. Miss Pollard was a long-time friend of the family; clearly she and Mr. Bancroft had grown up in one another's presence. I was still the outsider, though I hoped I wouldn't be for long. A tightness formed in my middle. Why did that thought make me feel so anxious?

Focusing on the music notes, I shook the thought away. My relationship with the women aside, I *needed* Mr. Bancroft to propose. Noah's drinking was growing worse by and by, and I had no other option available to me. If the worst were to occur, he would likely leave Charlotte and me both penniless and homeless. It was up to me to get ahead of the trouble we faced.

I had made the right choice in accepting Mr. Bancroft's invitation. I refused to wed another man who cared less for me than I did for him, and Mr. Bancroft was generous in his regard and his attention. Furthermore, each day spent in his company assured me more and more that he would not alter into a monster after we wed. Mr. Bancroft was security. He was constancy. Of both things, my life had been lacking for far too long.

An image of Frank's face passed through my mind. My thoughts were unfair. Frank had never been a monster. He simply had not cared for me. He was a man prone to anger when on leave from fighting Napoleon, but we were amidst war. He could have been different if our situations were changed, or so I told myself.

The men entered the room and I glanced up, catching Mr. Bancroft's beaming eye as he crossed toward the instrument.

He grasped his hands behind his back, standing just to the side of the pianoforte. "I have boasted considerably about your skill, Mrs. Wheeler. I cannot wait for you to stun the crowd."

My fingers fumbled on the keys, coming to a halt as I sat up. He was in earnest, though it surprised me. He seemed to care quite a lot about impressing the other guests, and spoke as though my abilities might aid in his consequence. "Of course, sir. What should I play?"

"Anything, my dear. Anything that will showcase your exquisite voice. I have dreamed of it these last few years."

Nodding, I put away the music as Mr. Bancroft called to the room, informing them of my presentation. The quiet settled on my shoulders with the weight of Mr. Bancroft's expectations and I swallowed. Laying shaking fingers upon the keys, I closed my eyes and began to play from memory a song I had often recited when called upon during my Season in London.

I performed with abandon, instantly transported back to a less complicated time, a less complicated me. Before my parents were killed in a carriage accident on their way to visit the Kensington gardens. Before I'd been ripped from the middle of my first Season. Before I'd been planted at my aunt's dreary home in Northumberland with no friends or connections. Why I had become a ward of Aunt Mary and my sister, Charlotte, had become a ward of our brother was unclear to me. Perhaps my father had not intended to separate us but only forgot to change his will. It would not have been unlike him to have forgotten.

My fingers played the final notes, drawing out the song with my voice far after the pianoforte completed its tune.

Enthusiastic clapping reached my ears and I was stunned back to the present, turning to find the party watching me in my moment of vulnerability. The women all wore shocked expressions on their faces, though Mrs. Bancroft was more guarded than either of the younger women. The men looked pleased, though perhaps Mr. Pollard least of all. He clearly cared little for my singing, but I was pleased to realize his disapproval did not bother me in the slightest. He was likely only bothered that I had interrupted his nap.

"Encore!" Mr. Peterson shouted, clapping once again.

"Yes, do play again, Mrs. Wheeler," Mr. Bancroft added, his voice extraordinarily pleased.

"I should not like to monopolize the instrument. Perhaps Miss Pollard would like to play?"

Her eyes widened as her face paled. Had I said the wrong thing? "Or Mrs. Haley?" I amended.

Mrs. Haley stood. "I would love to."

I moved to a chair that sat at the side of the group, alone. Mrs. Haley began to play a light melody as Lord Stallsbury pushed away from the wall and came to sit beside me. I expected praise, it was what most people would have expected in the situation, and I was somewhat miffed when he failed to speak.

"Do you enjoy music, my lord?" I whispered.

He nodded, his gaze trained on Mrs. Haley.

Several moments passed before he spoke again. "You are quite talented."

Warmth pooled in my stomach and I tried to suppress the smile his words ignited, particularly since I had requested the praise myself.

"And thus you've been told time and again, I'd imagine," he continued. "Though you do not need to hear it from me, allow me to reiterate that you have a gift. I look forward to hearing you perform again."

"Thank you," I said softly.

He leaned in slightly. "And how does your injured foot fare? I imagine it is, in fact, hurt?"

"It is bruised," I confirmed. "Though I think I will live."

"Bravo!" Mr. Bancroft clapped, startling me. Mrs. Haley curtseyed, closing the pianoforte with a thud and resuming her seat beside her mother.

"I've got a mind to play a game of whist," Lord Stallsbury said, his brown eyes locked on my own. "Would you care to join me if I can entice another pair?"

I nodded and he stood, moving toward the group seated near the sofas. Mr. Bancroft stood, as well as Miss Pollard, and we assembled around a card table on the opposite side of the room.

Lord Stallsbury refused to look at me while he dealt the cards and I had the distinct feeling that he desired to say much, and therefore said nothing. Mr. Bancroft more than made up for the marquess's lack of conversation and he and Miss Pollard shared their favorite aspects of the county.

"Rowland Vale would be a glorious setting for a picnic if we can but force this rain to cease," Miss Pollard said, gazing into her hand of cards.

"Perhaps we shall watch the weather for an opportunity to go," Mr. Bancroft said, eyeing me. "Rowland boasts a glorious set of ancient ruins that was once an abbey, though now is little more than a pile of stones. The history is quite rich. Should you enjoy that, Mrs. Wheeler?"

"Indeed, I would. I have always appreciated a decent set of ruins."

"How very British of you," Lord Stallsbury droned. "If that is the case then you would love my house. I live in a historically rich pile of stones myself."

"But you live in a *castle*, my lord!" Miss Pollard said, awed. "You cannot be so callous as to call it a pile of stones!"

He eyed her as Mr. Bancroft took his turn, and then laid down a card of his own. "It is a drafty place. Grand in design and perhaps even in theory, but the reality of growing up in a castle was hardly what the fairy tales depict."

The hard lines on his face were unmoving. It was clearly a topic that he cared to avoid.

"Your gown is exquisite, Miss Pollard," I said, waiting for her to lay down her card before I could play my own. "Did you have it made in London?"

She glanced down, screwing up her face. "This old thing? I can't quite remember. I've got so many of them, I can never recall where they were obtained."

"How enjoyable that must be for you." I attempted to swallow my bitterness. Had I been successful? I set down my card, glancing up to catch Lord Stallsbury's searching face.

"My sister orders hers in Town as well," Mr. Bancroft put in, dutifully following my change of direction. "Says there isn't a talented seamstress to be found around here."

"Though she lives in London," Lord Stallsbury added, "so that is not at all strange."

"Where did you get yours?" Miss Pollard asked, the sweetness of her tone belying her false innocence. Clearly, I was not wearing the latest fashion, and Miss Pollard knew this.

"It was a combined effort," I explained. I was not about to announce to any of these people that I had rebirthed an old gown with fresh embroidery and an altered style.

Miss Pollard eyed my gown and opened her mouth to speak when Lord Stallsbury cut her off, saying, "It is lovely, regardless of the modiste from which it came. I find that the blue is very becoming on you, Mrs. Wheeler."

"I concur," Mr. Bancroft said heartily.

I dipped my head, attempting to hide my blush. The men were kind, to be sure, but had not helped me to find a friend in Miss Pollard. The woman's glare was faintly evident before I'd dipped my head, and I could feel the warmth of her dislike clearly. I felt like this woman's rival, though I could not precisely say why.

I had not made an enemy, exactly. But I certainly had not made a friend, either.

CHAPTER 7

"**A**re we to keep meeting this way?"

The voice in the dark startled me, causing me to drop my candle on the rug. The flight had extinguished its flame and I knelt, feeling around for it on the smooth wooden floor. I was grateful for the distraction to give me a moment to calm my breathing.

Lord Stallsbury lit a lamp on the table beside his chair and I glanced up, surprised to find him fully dressed and once again, sitting in the dark. His dark hair disheveled, he looked tired about the eyes and in the set of his mouth.

"I had not expected to find you again," I said, picking up the candle and pulling myself to stand. I crossed to the back of the wingback chair I had sat in during our previous meeting, resting my hands on it. "This is not the library," I said at once. The lamp lit the room sufficiently to see that the only case containing books was near the door. The heavy wooden furniture and large desk at the far end inferred a different sort of room altogether.

"No, it is not," he agreed. "It is Bancroft's study."

My cheeks warmed at once. It was a private space belonging

to the master of the house and I had breached it twice in the night, believing myself alone. Utter mortification filtered through me.

"I have been looking for the library," I defended.

"That would explain why you were reading a book then, last night."

I gave him a wry smile. "And this being a study would certainly explain why I only found boring books."

He mocked affront. "So you admit you care nothing for farming?"

"I shall leave that to the professionals. I have only sought out some light reading to better pass the evenings."

"Our company is not sufficient?"

"I was referring to the time when all others are sleeping."

"All others but ourselves," he said softly.

"I suppose that is true. What is keeping you awake this evening, my lord?" I circled around the chair, lowering myself on the plush cushion. His dinner jacket was open to reveal a fine waistcoat; his cravat had been removed, but that was the only indication that he had made himself comfortable.

I couldn't help but wonder if he'd remained dressed for my sake.

"More of the same." He crossed one ankle languidly over the other knee.

"And have you grown closer to a conclusion?" I inquired.

"I have not yet decided if I shall choose to marry or not, if that is what you mean. Or if the woman who drew me here is going to be a proper fit."

I took in a long, deep breath. I was defying convention with these frank questions. It was outside polite manners to inquire so, and he had every right to put me utterly in my place and storm from the room; neither of which he seemed inclined to do. His actions begged the question: did he wish to speak to me about these things? Perhaps he desired a listening ear who had no direct attachment to the things with which he struggled. I certainly was not interested in marrying him. Perhaps my objectivity appealed to him.

"You must know what you would prefer to do, or this would not be such a difficult thing to decide," I said. "What is it that holds you back?"

"My family."

That came easily. "In what way?"

His voice was quiet. I saw in him the vulnerable young boy that he likely once was. "I dare not disappoint them. I care not for my father's opinion, but for my mother, Cameron, and Rosalynn. It would hurt me deeply if I hurt them."

"Do you mean Lord Cameron and Lady Rosalynn?" I asked. Surely it could not be a coincidence that I knew two titled siblings with the same names. "I had the pleasure of meeting them only last month in Shropshire."

He looked at me then. "What were they doing in Shropshire?"

"Visiting Miss Hurst at Corden Hall. How would it hurt them if you were cut off? You would still inherit eventually."

He nodded. "I didn't know she lived there."

He had not answered my question. I remained silent, waiting.

"I know that Cameron is happy. He is married now, and they are content. They've only just bought an estate in Northumberland, not far from the castle. Neither of my siblings would want their penniless brother to hang onto them, stay for long periods of time. I would become the poor relation."

"Then you must decide if you would prefer to handle the consequences or simply acquiesce."

He shook his head. "I cannot depend upon my brother in such a way."

"Then your answer is clear," I said simply.

He ran a hand through his hair. "It is not so easy. Regardless of my choice I am depending upon another person in some form. There is no winning for me here." Standing, he paced the length of the room, his long legs crossing the distance in few strides. After a round about the room he dropped into the chair again, holding his face in his hands.

"Would you like to hold a competition?" I asked, trepidation running the length of my body.

He glanced up slowly, his brow pulled together in confusion as his dark eyes searched mine. "What is the nature of the competition?"

"Marriage."

That seemed to shock him. I hurried to continue before he could think I was propositioning him. "We have both come here with essentially the same end goal in mind: marriage. I have come to meet Mr. Bancroft's family and acquaint ourselves to decide if we would suit. You came with the understanding that you must choose a wife or be cut off. And if I followed you correctly, you were enticed here with the possibility of a match with Miss Pollard. Regardless of your uncertainty, I feel that you know which path you are going to take. Whomever can secure an engagement first, wins."

"What would I win?"

I laughed. "So sure of yourself, my lord?"

His face was serious, but the set of his mouth was bent in a self-deprecating smile. "I need only walk upstairs and request a visit with Mr. Pollard and I can have a marriage agreement written within the hour."

My eyebrows hitched up. "You've made your choice quickly. Perhaps we ought to wait until the morning, though. It wouldn't do to frighten your father-in-law into submission."

"What will I win?" he repeated, a gleam evident in his eye. Clearly I had hit upon his competitive nature.

"To be honest, I had not yet thought of that."

He leaned back in his chair again, clasping his hands before him, his mind clearly working through the problem. "If you win, you shall have my horse. Do not deny that you were eyeing him while we were outside."

My cheeks warmed. Had I been so obvious? "I was, but then what would you ride?"

He waved his hand, pushing the argument away as though it did not matter. "I can obtain another horse."

"And if you win?"

"If I win, I may choose something of yours."

I scoffed. "But what? My lord, I have very little. I certainly have nothing to tempt you."

He watched me then, unspeaking. What had I said? Surely he did not desire my pearl earrings? They were the only thing I had received from my mother and the only thing I owned of any value. I refused to part with them.

"You will sing for me."

Smiling, I tilted my head. "My lord, I sang for you this evening."

"No, you sang. But not for *me*."

Confused, I shook my head. "My song for a horse? That is hardly a fair wager."

"It is completely fair when one would consider the situation of the giver. I will give a horse, something of which I do not hurt to part with. You will give a song, of which you have infinite reserve."

I shook my head. In theory, it made sense. "How are we to take this seriously if neither of us has very much to lose?"

He grinned, coming to a stand. "Because I very much like to win."

CHAPTER 8

L ord Stallsbury sat at the breakfast table quite alone. He stood as I entered and I found the lack of shadows which would have been cast by a single candle unnerving. I had grown used to being shrouded in darkness when alone in the marquess's company. Though I could not deny how much I appreciated his handsomeness in the light of day. His features were quite pleasing, and he was well-proportioned, his hair making up in height for the particular point to his chin.

"Now that I know you are Lord Cameron's brother," I said, "it is not the least surprising. You look very much alike."

He picked up a roll and spread jam over it. "Yes, so we've been told. Both of my brothers closely resemble me."

"And who is the other?" I questioned, taking a bite of my coddled egg. I had only met the one, and of course his sister, Lady Rosalynn.

"Geoff," he answered quietly. "Though he died some years ago."

My next bite paused en route to my mouth and I glanced up at Lord Stallsbury. "I am sorry, my lord. I didn't know."

He smiled perfunctorily. "You are not at fault. It is not a

great secret. He was meant to inherit the dukedom, you know. But now it will fall to me when my father dies."

Clearly, I did not, for I didn't even know of his existence. Though now it was beginning to make sense why the Lord Stallsbury before me did not match the reputation I'd heard so much about. Could Geoff be the brother that had lived in such a profligate way?

"How long ago did he die?" I asked. My Season in London was five years ago. That is when I would have heard the worst of the rumors, to be sure.

"It has been just four years. It was a duel. Quite reckless, actually. He did not even care overly much for the woman whose honor he had called into question. He was merely too prideful to turn down the challenge."

I itched to reach forward and clasp his hand but I knew it was not done. He feigned indifference, and perhaps time had allowed him to distance himself from the pain, but losing a brother and gaining a title at once could not have been an easy thing to bear.

Mr. Bancroft entered the room then, on the arm of his mother, and I was exceedingly grateful I had kept my hands near myself.

"A lovely morning," Mr. Bancroft said, filling a plate at the sidebar and seating himself beside me. "Perhaps we might go for a walk today?"

"As long as Mrs. Wheeler does not bring the rain," Mr. Peterson said, entering that moment with Miss Pollard directly behind him.

"You cannot believe that, man," Mr. Bancroft said. He was growing irritated, that was evident. Though why it bothered him so greatly was beyond me. I knew Mr. Peterson was exceedingly facetious. Not a fault, entirely. It was nothing more than personal taste in humor, but clearly it was one that Mr. Bancroft did not share.

"You might borrow an umbrella," I said to Mr. Peterson, ignoring Mr. Bancroft's incredulous face. "Then you shall be armed for the possibility."

He paused, regarding me. "So you admit that you could potentially bring the rain."

I could not help but laugh. "No, sir. I admit that rain in and of itself is a possibility. We do live in England, after all."

Mr. Pollard entered the room and the topic moved to more neutral ground, but I could not shake the unease that Mr. Bancroft's gaze created within me. He was displeased with me, though I knew not why. Yet I had a feeling that I would find out soon enough. He had an uneasy way of watching me whenever I was not quite acting with precise care.

"I trust you slept well?" I said, veering him onto a more neutral path.

"Yes, thank you," he answered. "And yourself, Mrs. Wheeler?"

"Beautifully, thank you." After I returned to my room, of course. I had been so tired that I collapsed upon my bedclothes and fell asleep at once, despite the discomfort of my corset.

"I was hoping to take a trip into Gersham today to search out new ribbons," Miss Pollard cut in from across the table. She'd claimed a seat beside Lord Stallsbury.

He shot me a little grin before turning to her. "I should love to escort you into Gersham today, Miss Pollard. The sun looks quite inviting, do you not think?"

"Very inviting, indeed," she said, obviously pleased by his attentiveness.

Mrs. Haley wiped her mouth, setting her napkin in her lap. "I saw the loveliest little cap in the window just last week. Perhaps we should check and see if it is still available."

"Certainly," Mr. Bancroft answered. If the way he cared for his sister was any indication of how he meant to care for any woman in his life, then I had made the correct choice. Even the way he had thoughtfully protected Miss Pollard from the rain, whom he clearly considered to be someone like a sister, and how he weighed his mother's opinions when choosing a wife, indicated his superior sensitivity to women.

Charlotte and I would be protected. We would be safe. That was infinitely more important than a decent sense of humor. Mr. Bancroft did not have the rugged nature or dashing scar along his cheek like my novel heroes, but he was real. And that mattered significantly more.

"Are we willing to risk the rain if Mrs. Wheeler attends?" Mr. Peterson asked.

Mr. Bancroft harrumphed. "Poppycock, and you know it. Curses are not real."

"So you say." Mr. Peterson turned playful eyes on me. "But mark my words, the outing shall end in rain if Mrs. Wheeler is to come."

———

"Do not fret yourself, dear," Mr. Bancroft said, coming to stand beside me. "No one truly blames you for the rain. You said so this morning, we do live in England, after all."

He patted my hand where it sat on the windowsill of the haberdashery. Mrs. Bancroft, Mrs. Haley and Miss Pollard were admiring various lengths of ribbon hanging in the opposite window, but I could not tear my gaze from the panes streaming with rain. It had been a gloriously bright morning when we set out for Gersham. We had hardly made it into town when the clouds rolled in, bringing cold rain with them.

"Now what shall you choose today?" he asked. "My treat."

"Oh, I couldn't." I glanced down at the half boots adorning my feet. I had yet to discover the identity of my mysterious benefactor, but Mr. Bancroft was the likeliest and most obvious suspect; until we were engaged, more gifts were far from appropriate.

"But I insist."

"It is kind of you, but I must refuse. I shall help your sister choose a color that suits her," I said, as though I had any authority on the matter.

Approaching the women, I regretted my choice immediately.

"I do not know why she thinks herself worthy," Mrs. Bancroft was saying, her back securely toward me. I installed myself behind a cabinet stocked with fabric.

"Mother, please," Mrs. Haley begged, "now is not the time. If William chooses her then what right have you to say anything on the matter? It is his choice."

"As the woman remaining in the house with William and his wife, I should think I have *some* little say on the matter," she answered acerbically, turning away from them to look at the ribbons hanging in the other window.

I stepped back quickly, concerning myself with an array of velvet and doing my utmost not to disturb them. Mrs. Bancroft was not unreasonable in her concerns. I had little to bring to a marriage, in dowry or status.

"Do not let her bother you," a deep voice said just behind me. I stilled, his breath so close I felt it on my ear. Lord Stallsbury.

"Her complaints are valid," I whispered.

"Her selfishness is not."

I turned my head slightly, trying to mask my surprise when I caught deep brown eyes and a lock of dark hair so close behind me.

"You possess more qualities than a hundred brainless debutantes. Do not let the musings of that insufferable woman deter you from your goal. Mr. Bancroft would be lucky to have you for his wife."

A chill swept over me. I felt Lord Stallsbury's lack the moment he stepped away. Fingering a lilac colored velvet, I tried to appear as though my emotions had not just been put through a butter churn.

"That is a lovely color," Mrs. Haley said, coming up beside me.

I flinched, dropping the ribbon and wiping my perspiring fingers along the skirt of my gown. "Yes, quite lovely. Though I fear I would have no use for it."

I turned away, crossing toward the door where the majority of our party stood in wait. Mrs. Bancroft waited beside Miss Pollard, their arms snugly entwined.

Mr. Peterson stepped into the haberdashery, forcing the women to back into the room. He lifted two black objects, searching the shop. Grinning when his eyes found my own, he said, "I've obtained umbrellas!"

CHAPTER 9

The party was nestled in the drawing room with multiple card tables set up for play, a large fire roaring in the hearth and a table set with hot tea. I ensconced myself at a writing table near the window and began drafting a letter to Charlotte I still had not managed to write. I dared not mention the competition or presence of Lord Stallsbury, for fear she would mention it to Miss Hurst. It was not a secret, I was sure, but I had the inclination that he needed his privacy at this time.

He approached my table. "Can I tempt you in a round of whist?"

"Perhaps when I complete my letter," I said, glancing behind him to the rain-strewn window. "I am not quite finished yet."

He nodded, though he did not move away. "I could send a servant for some toasted cheese, if you'd like."

The thoughtful gesture surprised me. I glanced up, quite expecting to find him grinning, but his guileless face was modest and dull, as though he was affecting that he cared little for my answer. If I had more consequence, I would imagine that Lord Stallsbury was feeling vulnerable.

"I am quite content at the moment, but I thank you for the regard." It was pleasant to have one's insignificant musings remembered by another. I found my heart lightened by his thoughtfulness, small as it might be.

A loud snore interrupted us and I jumped, blotting ink on the letter. Drat Mr. Pollard and his constant roaring. However did one man sleep so much?

"I will leave you to it," Lord Stallsbury said, eyeing my blotted paper before walking away.

The butler came to the door to announce a guest. I hurried to complete my letter, informing Charlotte of the dashing horses the gentleman rode and the fantastic little duck pond—I could not refrain from adding the anecdote of Miss Pollard's fear of the ducks themselves. Smiling to myself, I folded and sealed the letter, spinning on my chair in time to see Mr. Bancroft's guests enter the room.

"Miss Thornton, Mr. Thornton, welcome! I believed you weren't going to make it."

The note dropped from my fingers, hitting the floor.

"Thornton?" My voice hardly rose above a whisper. He was busy greeting Mr. Bancroft and the other guests, his face crinkling in pleasant satisfaction. I cleared my throat and tried again, louder this time. "Thornton?"

He turned at once, eyes widened, his mouth drooping in shock. "Mrs. Wheeler, whatever are you doing here?"

He approached me and I held my hand out, tears springing to my eyes of their own accord. I dashed them away with the back of my wrist, smiling at the familiar face that brought to surface feelings equal in delight and difficulty.

Kissing the back of my hand, he held it in both of his. "How have you been?" he asked softly. "You are still Mrs. Wheeler, I presume?"

"I am." I nodded. "Have you brought your sister with you? I am delighted. You know I have heard so much about her."

He grinned. "Yes, allow me to introduce you."

I swallowed, apprehension growing as I crossed the room on Thornton's arm. This woman was bound to hate me. She was predisposed to despise me. I took a breath to calm my racing heart, clenching my hands to quit their shaking.

"Sarah, this is Mrs. Wheeler."

I curtsied, coming up to look in her deep green eyes. Light brown hair curled into tiny ringlets and gathered upon her head framed a perfectly heart-shaped face. She smiled beatifically, stepping forward and dipping her head.

"I am so honored to make your acquaintance," she said. "I have long wondered what you looked like. My brother's descriptions are not always reliable. Though he was correct in his assessment of your beauty, to be sure."

Warmth flooded my cheeks and I very pointedly ignored Thornton standing beside me. I could not bear to look into his eyes now and see a reflection of the man I had met the day I married Frank.

"Are you planning to stay?" I asked Miss Thornton, forcing myself to not think of that day, or how Frank had once considered marrying her, but chose me instead. They'd never reached a formal agreement, but I could imagine the disappointment she had felt at the announcement of our engagement, nonetheless.

"Yes, we've come for the house party. We are late, of course, but we were unsure if we would be able to get away from our aunt's house until the moment we left."

I nodded. Suddenly the remaining occupants in the room came into focus. Mr. Bancroft and Lord Stallsbury stood just behind Miss Thornton. Mrs. Bancroft, Mrs. Haley and Miss Pollard remained on the sofa to my left. Nerves raced up and down my spine. It was too much, my worlds colliding in such a manner. I took a breath and found that my lungs would not fill satisfactorily. "If you'll excuse me," I said to Mr. Bancroft, willing my voice to sound natural, "I am going to rest for the afternoon. I shall return in time for dinner."

I dipped a curtsy and forced myself to walk calmly from the room. The moment I reached the stairs I climbed them with all of the speed I possessed.

"Mrs. Wheeler!"

I turned at once, missing the step and falling hard on the stairs. Thundered footsteps raced toward me and I pushed myself up.

"Are you hurt?" Lord Stallsbury asked, picking up my fingers and pulling me to a stand. I had hit my shin on the wooden stair and it hurt something fierce, but I was not about to say so aloud. I needed to absent myself at once.

Blinking away tears, I tried to smile, pulling my hand free of his warm grip. "I am fine, sir."

I turned to go when he stopped me.

"Yes?" I asked, glancing down at his hand gripping my own.

He released me immediately, his brow furrowing. "You are shaking."

"I need to rest."

"Very well. You forgot this." He extended the letter I had written to Charlotte. "Shall I frank it for you?"

I knew what the marquess meant; he was offering to post my letter. But hearing my husband's name was my final undoing. I nodded, words failing me, and turned away, running up the stairs heedless of decorum or proper manners. I did not stop or curtsy to the Peer, I merely fled. I simply needed to process the recent events and the feelings they brought up.

One small nap and I would be right as rain once again.

If gathering in the drawing room for dinner was difficult with Miss Pollard in attendance, Miss Thornton made it positively horrifying. I donned the cream gown with embroidered leaves and my pearl earrings. I had felt regal and elegant in my bedchamber, yet dull and shabby when faced with such esteemed beauty. Miss Thornton absolutely shone. Her gown draped over her in waves of luscious silk, and her hair was a precise confection of tight curls and delicate jeweled pins.

What was more, she sat near the fireplace drawing attention from every ear in the room. When faced with such beauty and charisma, I could not see why Frank chose me over her.

"Mrs. Wheeler," she called, her smile revealing a decent set of teeth. She patted the sofa cushion beside her. "Come, sit."

I obeyed, settling myself beside her.

"Are you feeling refreshed?"

"Yes," I said, trying to match her smile with one of equal brilliance. I feared I was only baring my teeth at her. "I am feeling much more the thing."

"Splendid. I cannot wait to learn more from you. I feel I should have known you before now."

"Quite so. Are you familiar with the rest of the party?" I asked, attempting to deflect the attention from myself.

She nodded. "I've known Lord Stallsbury an age, of course."

I looked over sharply to where he stood near the fire with Thornton. It was true that he looked comfortable, as if he was speaking to an old friend and not a new acquaintance. "How do you know Lord Stallsbury?"

"We live near his family home. My brother has been a friend of his for years."

I nodded. Of course they lived near one another. I had met my husband in Northumberland. He and Thornton were childhood friends and maintained a relationship close enough to warrant Thornton's visits whenever Frank came home on leave. The two had spent many evenings playing cards. But that was all in the past. Thornton was a gamester, but he was loyal and caring. He had been a stalwart and surprising support when I had faced Frank's death.

I did not know what I would have done if Thornton had not arrived to handle the business elements of it all. The funeral, burial, and sale of the estate were all far above my reach. He had taken over the duty of obtaining everything he could, and then subsequently using it to pay off Frank's debts, of which there had been many. I'd hardly had the stamina to dress in my widows weeds and pack my belongings to return to Noah's house and my dear Charlotte.

The butler announced dinner then and I moved through the motions as though I watched myself interact with the others from some perch above the room. What would this do to the party, to have Thornton and his sister present? Would Mr. Bancroft begin asking questions that brought up my unsavory marriage?

I swallowed, feeling the blood drain from my face. I feared I was about to lose everything, and all for the sake of a dratted house party. Mrs. Bancroft would never give her blessing if she knew of my poverty and unsuitable husband, surely. There was little more I could do to secure my place as Mr. Bancroft's wife, but I needed to do it now. I had no choice if I was to save Charlotte and myself from our deteriorating home and absent brother.

I simply had to receive a proposal from Mr. Bancroft, and the sooner the better.

CHAPTER 10

"But surely you've got plans to invite some of the gentry here. How else will our Mrs. Wheeler acquaint herself with local society?" Miss Thornton positively pouted, her delicate eyebrows drawn together in confusion. She was intelligent, and her knowing eyes left me uneasy. I could not quite make out whether she was mocking me or speaking in earnest. In the end I chose to assume the best, but guard myself against her worst.

Mrs. Bancroft chortled. "Whatever would the local gentry have to say on the matter? My son has been highly sought after for years. He is a prize regardless of the quality of—"

"*Mother*," Mr. Bancroft cut in, his face flushed beet red. He stood from the plush chair he occupied near his mother and crossed to the fire. The drawing room was nearly stifling and the hour late. The men had lingered quite a while over their port. Due, I am sure, to our newest additions to the party. Thornton likely hadn't seen his friends in some time.

Miss Thornton had, it seemed, chosen to take me under her wing. When Mrs. Haley informed her immediately of the potential connection between Mr. Bancroft and myself, she had set right to discussing the merits of the merger and how we could group together as women to bring Mr. Bancroft to the sticking point more speedily.

Mrs. Bancroft hadn't seemed very pleased with the idea at all.

"I believe the quality of society matters little when the marriage match is well enough," I explained. I'd known nearly no one in the small town in which Frank and I had resided. Though, I couldn't deny that had added to my loneliness. I chose not to admit as much, however, as it wasn't exactly a point in my favor in this particular conversation.

"Of course," Miss Thornton gushed, laying a palm upon her heart. "I would not suggest otherwise. I merely refer to when the marriage does not turn out exactly as one might hope. It helps to have friends."

I went cold. How much about my marriage did she know? If Frank complained to Thornton, the man easily—and innocently —could have relayed information to his sister.

Mrs. Bancroft eyed me deliberately. "I have not missed a London Season these twenty-five years at least. And our time in Bancroft Hill is restful and rejuvenating. The people here are varied enough for my tastes, and I'm sure it'll do for any woman that William chooses to take to wife."

The matter settled, Mrs. Haley said, "Mrs. Wheeler, won't you sing for us this evening?"

Miss Pollard glanced up quickly, a smile turning her lips. She had been mostly silent and sulky since the moment dinner began and I was sure Miss Thornton was pressing on her nerves. In that, at least, we could be united. "Yes, Mrs. Wheeler, please do."

Mr. Bancroft added, "I should love to hear you sing once more."

I stood, nodding acquiescence. "Very well."

Lord Stallsbury, Mr. Peterson and Thornton had brought

their conversation into the drawing room and were yet standing near the piano discussing something amongst themselves. "I apologize," I said, coming to stand beside them, "but you are blocking my way."

"Are you to sing for us?" Mr. Peterson asked.

I nodded.

He turned to Thornton. "You are in for a treat, old boy."

Lord Stallsbury turned to Thornton. "But surely you've heard Mrs. Wheeler sing before. You were previously acquainted with her husband, yes?"

"Can't say that I have." He shrugged. Turning to me, he grinned. "You never sang for me and Frank together, at least."

I ignored the final remark, feigning occupation with the sheet music. It was an act, and when the men dispersed, I warmed up my fingers on the keys a moment before delving into another song I knew by heart.

It was a slow ballad I learned in the moments of solitude when Aunt Mary had left me to my own devices. Which, in truth, was very seldom. She had been a stifling, controlling force of a woman who demanded my every moment of time to do her bidding. My young age and Aunt Mary's oppressive nature combined to push me into Frank's arms. I liked to think I would have made a different choice in husband had I not been battling grief and feeling such desperation to be rid of my aunt, but Frank had made me believe that he loved me dearly. And what young woman did not want to believe that?

After the wedding, he'd wanted nearly nothing to do with me. The change had been so sudden and direct I had believed myself to be responsible. After years of reflection though, I could not help but wonder what it was that caused the change in him. For surely it could not have been solely my fault.

I delved deeper into the music, allowing my song to carry away the frustrations brought to light by the Thorntons' appearance.

The room was positively silent when I finished, and I rested my hands in my lap, turning toward the group. They broke into applause at once and I watched Thornton pick up his jaw and join in.

As I stood, Thornton appeared by my side. "Good gads, Mrs. Wheeler, wherever did you learn to sing like that?"

"I've sung all my life, sir."

He scoffed, his eyebrows hitched up like thick caterpillars in the center of his forehead. "Did Frank know?"

"Actually, no," I answered, avoiding Lord Stallsbury's burning gaze not far behind Thornton's shoulder. "I do not believe he did."

"I have just the thing!" The room quieted, our attention turning unanimously toward Miss Thornton and her outburst. "Why do we not roll up the rugs and have a dance? Mrs. Wheeler, you played the pianoforte superbly, I am sure you could find a little tune to lead us along?"

I gazed into her calculating eyes a moment longer before nodding. "I would love to." In present company, I much preferred the idea of playing over dancing.

A grin spread slowly along her lips. "Splendid."

A few footmen entered the room, undoubtedly called upon by the butler, and began shifting furniture and rolling up rugs.

"You don't have to play, you know." I jumped, turning to find Miss Pollard standing directly behind me.

"It is no matter. I truly do not mind."

She frowned. "She cannot barge in here and begin controlling us all as though we are her playthings."

If I didn't know better, I would have assumed that Miss Pollard was fighting the urge to stomp her foot.

"I cannot like it," she pouted. "And I do not see how you can either when she clearly has designs on Mr. Bancroft."

She flounced away and I watched her go, my mouth agape. I shut it quickly and turned for the sheet music, flipping through it to find a song to play. I had not seen a single indication that Miss Thornton had any designs on Mr. Bancroft. But I was determined to watch for the signs now.

The consensus was a waltz, which was easy enough, and the group paired themselves off, forming a circle to begin the promenade as I began playing the music.

I was fairly talented at playing music without watching my fingers and spent a good deal of time observing the couples. Miss Pollard and Mr. Bancroft looked comfortable with one another, her smile positively gleeful. If she felt it necessary to warn me against Miss Thornton's designs against my potential husband, what did she expect me to make of *her?* I could only find comfort, I supposed, in the clear evidence that if Mr. Bancroft desired a union with Miss Pollard, it likely would have already occurred. It was my belief that he did not even consider her an option.

Miss Thornton partnered with Lord Stallsbury and they were a positively regal couple, swaying to the music in sync with the rest of the dancers but achieving a mastery that came down to inherent talent. Thornton partnered Mrs. Haley, and Mr. Pollard was kind enough to wake up from his post-dinner nap long enough to partner Mrs. Bancroft.

As the song came to a close, each of the couples bowed to one another and then turned to clap toward the pianoforte.

"Shall we have another?" Miss Pollard asked. She had quickly turned from a concerned friend to an accomplice of Miss Thornton, though that did not surprise me one bit.

"I have done my duty, but I should love to see you young people continue to dance," Mrs. Bancroft said. "It does this old heart some good to see the younger set enjoying themselves in such wholesome activity. Mrs. Wheeler," she said, directing her false smile at me, "you are positively unrivaled at the pianoforte, I cannot imagine how we came so blessed to count you in our party."

I took her hint as clearly as she laid it out for me. She would like me to continue playing so I might not have the opportunity to dance. I did not mind. I usually chose to sit behind the instrument when given the option. But being stationed there by the mother of the man I was intending to marry did rankle some.

"A country dance?" I inquired. The group agreed and formed a set. Mr. Bancroft with his sister, Mr. Peterson with Miss Thornton, and Lord Stallsbury with Miss Pollard.

I played a lively tune, quite livelier than it was intended, and it appeared to tire the company.

"Shall we have a quadrille next?" Mr. Bancroft asked, his breath coming in heaves.

"Or perhaps another waltz?" Mrs. Haley asked. "Come, Mrs. Wheeler, allow me to trade places with you."

"I am quite content here," I said, deferring her concern.

She crossed toward me, her eyes a steel I had yet to see from her. "I insist," she said through her teeth.

No sooner had I acquiesced than Mr. Bancroft requested to partner me and led me into the small circle that created our dance. Lord Stallsbury was once again with Miss Thornton and Mr. Peterson partnered Miss Pollard.

"You have such musical talent," Mr. Bancroft said, leading me into the promenade. "I could imagine that one might grow used to hearing your lovely voice every evening."

"I used to perform for my parents nightly," I confessed. "Though I have never been fond of public performances and did my best to avoid them in Town."

"It is such a shame to hide such a lovely talent. It is quite the sort of thing which should be displayed for all to hear."

I blushed. Perhaps if I had sung more in London then Mr. Bancroft would have proposed before my parents' untimely death. We could have been engaged, thus allowing me to stay behind in London and avoid my dreadful time at Aunt Mary's. I might have had a husband by choice, rather than desperation.

Though if he *had* come to the sticking point, I likely would have refused him. One tends to see the past through a perfect lens, but without the wisdom I'd gained since, it was impossible to know what I might have done.

"I wouldn't mind if that became a regular occurrence," he said quietly.

My singing? Nerves fluttered around my stomach as we danced. I was one step closer to obtaining the husband I sought, and I was a little closer to winning a horse for Charlotte as well.

I glanced at Lord Stallsbury, his rigid posture bending slightly to converse with his partner. She was particularly artful in the dip of her chin and flutter of her eyelashes and I swallowed a scoff before Mr. Bancroft could inquire what it was about.

Turning my attention back to the dance, I performed the familiar steps with a sense of release. Things were going well enough. I had dispatched a letter to Charlotte and thus should be hearing back from her by next week, and Mr. Bancroft had indicated he would appreciate my singing if it were a regular addition to his evenings, which was rather a blessing because I did not think I would be able to refrain from singing for long. Singing was a part of me—something I had missed for quite some time. Though there were periods of my life void of song, I did not think I could refrain forever.

CHAPTER 11

I stood outside my bedroom door, considering the merits of going down to the study. I was intelligent enough to admit that if I chose to go down, I was choosing to see Lord Stallsbury. While I enjoyed his conversation, I had no other motive, so would it still be considered a secret assignation? I paced the hallway, stopping before the stairs and turning back for my door.

No. No, it would not. My first justification was that neither of us had mentioned meeting together. In order to have a secret meeting, all parties surely had to predetermine a time and location and reveal their intention to meet. Another reason, most obviously, was that Lord Stallsbury and I were not in love. If we met to discuss our trials regarding *separate* lovers then there could be no real harm, could there?

Unless, of course, we were caught.

I halted. That was the root of my dilemma. If we were caught alone in the middle of the night then we would either be forced to wed, or our reputations would be in tatters. Or, realistically, both. I might be allowed more freedom as a widow, but gossip was gossip, and if we were discovered my name—and Charlotte's chances at finding a suitable husband—could be ruined.

So why were my feet moving down the stairs, my hand lightly trailing along the banister? I had foregone the candle this evening, choosing not to tempt fate by spilling light under any of the other guests' doors.

I did not know when my heart sped up, but the sight of light spilling from under the door of the study did something to the nerves within me and caused them to dance. I opened the door before I thought better of it, and at once panicked over my lack of caution.

The light could have been due to any number of men coming together in the evening for a nightcap before bed. I breathed utter relief when I saw Lord Stallsbury sitting alone, his legs stretched forward from his wingback chair. His cravat had been banished to the side table but his attire otherwise remained intact.

"You are late," he said, a playful edge to his tone, as I closed the door behind me and took my own seat, pulling my feet under me and tucking my skirt around my ankles.

"I did not know I was expected, sir."

"So says the woman who has been pacing the hallway for the last quarter-hour."

My cheeks went hot.

He smiled. "I believe the hallway is directly above this room. I have been apprised of your anxiety for the duration and am sorry to report that you've caused me a measure of my own."

"I apologize, my lord. It was not my intent."

He regarded me closely, his hands clasped over his stomach, his thumbs circling one another in rapid motion. "I also cannot help but wonder what made you choose to come?"

"The truth?" I lifted a shoulder. "I haven't the faintest."

His voice lowered. "Would you answer a question for me honestly if I were to ask it?"

My breath caught. "That would depend on the question, my lord."

He cast his gaze up. "Will you please quit calling me my lord?"

My chin rose and I tried to swallow my surprise, but I had not been effective if the grin on his face was any indication. "You cannot mean that. What am I meant to call you, Stallsbury?"

"Gads, no. Only my friends call me that."

That stung. I lifted one pale eyebrow. "And I am not your friend?"

"No," he answered simply. "You are something else."

Both of my eyebrows lifted. If he strayed in an inappropriate direction, I was ready to shoot out of there faster than a misdirected arrow. I did have the inclination, however, that Lord Stallsbury had more respect for me than that.

"Calm yourself," he said lazily. "I have no nefarious intentions. I only meant that you are not a friend, exactly. I would consider you a confidant."

I nodded. "I see. And have you brought me another dilemma to discuss this evening?"

"I suppose I have. I could not help but determine when we were in Gersham earlier that our competition was unfair. You were predisposed to come here and become engaged to Mr. Bancroft, and I had only come with the intention of considering Miss Pollard on the high recommendation from a friend. We did not begin on even ground, and we certainly do not have even ground now."

"Whatever will put us on even ground, sir? We cannot very well import more women for your choosing."

He watched me a moment before continuing, rubbing his hand under his chin. "I suppose I cannot complain too heavily. It just became even with the newest arrivals to the party."

My stomach clenched. He could not be serious. "You are considering Miss Thornton?"

"I suppose I am," he said, settling further into his chair. "She is beautiful, accomplished, and comes with wonderful connections. I've heard she has little dowry, of course, but I do not need wealth. I need a wife who understands her duties and shall leave me to take care of mine."

His points were valid; Miss Thornton would excel in the position he described. "And now you believe we are equally matched in our competition? Then whatever is the dilemma?"

"I suppose we are. I determined in the haberdashery that I was fooling myself to say I was considering Miss Pollard when I never would have intentionally courted her had I met her in London. The only reason I gave her any thought was the high praise I heard from the man who recommended her. But even then, I knew from the first day she lacks too many of the fine qualities I desire in a wife."

"I am glad to help you come to a decision about your future, sir, and I should think that you will have very happy parents by the end of this house party. Though they will be quite saddened to learn that they must eat the expense of purchasing you a new horse."

"We shall see," he said with a grin. "I find my taste for your song only increased this evening. Tell me, how could you marry a man and not allow him to discover your superior talent for music?"

I glanced down. This was a question I would have preferred unasked—something which could have been avoided had not Thornton arrived. "Music was not a part of my life then."

"I find that hard to believe. You radiate joy when you sing. How could you court and marry a man without any music?"

"Perhaps because I had no joy," I snapped.

We watched each other as the clock ticked on the other side of the room. I had not intended to explain myself but now I felt

I was left with little choice. Neither had I meant to show my anger. I had done a well enough job since the death of my parents to cool my emotions and refrain from outbursts; my marriage to Frank had only solidified that resolve.

"My lord, I—"

"Did I not ask you to drop the my lord? I am sick of the bowing and scraping. I am not even meant to be the marquess. I do not need the constant reminders. Especially from you."

Shock reverberated through me. "What do you mean, you were not meant to be the marquess? If I cannot refer to you as my lord, then what may I say?"

"As for the first," he said, looking toward the black window, "I was born a second son, which I believe I have told you. As for the second," he said, observing me closely, "you may call me Tarquin."

My spine straightened on its own. "I most certainly will not call you that."

"Whyever not? It is the name I was born with, the only one I have been able to claim throughout my entire life. It is the only thing connecting my past with the present."

Sudden pity washed through me and I saw in his hurt face a vulnerable boy—the one who grew up carefree, no concern for the title, estate and wealth he would one day inherit.

"What did you intend to do with your life before you became the marquess?"

He glanced at me sharply. "I considered joining the navy. I've always had a fascination with the ocean."

I had not expected that.

"You are surprised," he said. "Most of my family would be too, had they known. It was not something I was eager to announce."

"Whyever not? It is a worthy profession. Surely they would not oppose you."

"I only think they would not find *me* worthy enough to lead a ship full of men."

At once I saw the true root of the problem. The issue was not whether Lord Stallsbury's family deemed him worthy of leading a ship, it was whether he found himself worthy enough.

"Do you not think," I said gently, "that your family loves you, and would support whatever gentleman's profession you chose?"

He watched me, his mouth in a straight line, his eyes uncertain.

I continued, against my better judgment. "I believe if you had pursued a career in the navy it would have all worked out for good in the end."

"Do you believe that now?" he asked, his voice soft.

"You are going to be a duke now. You have no need for employment."

"I do not mean that. Do you believe that if one has good intentions, it shall all work out for the good?"

I laughed. He seemed so intent on the answer I would deliver that I felt pressure to relieve the tension in the room. "I am no master of theology. I only know I must rely on my own hope."

"And do you?"

"Have hope?" I asked, shaking my head in hopes that I might shake away my nerves as well. "Yes, I do. I must, for otherwise I would still be lonely and miserable."

He tilted his head to the side. "And you are not lonely and miserable now?"

He seemed to see me in a way that no other person did. Or perhaps it was the lateness of the hour and the lack of social graces between us. I stood, unclear on the direction of the conversation and uncomfortable with betraying too much about myself to a man I hardly knew.

"This conversation cannot be moving in a good direction. We should call it a night before—"

"Before I say something I regret?" he asked, his lips forming a sad smile. "I cannot help but consider both of our plights and the cause we have for being here, searching for a spouse. And yet, our friendship formed so naturally that I cannot help but wonder…"

I held my breath, standing before him as though awaiting conviction. He mentioned our equal need for marriage. It was a preposterous route to take, but…

Could the marquess be contemplating a union with me?

Shaking his head, he chuckled lightly. Sudden discomfort washed over us. "Nevermind. I see how it is impossible."

I cleared my throat. It was true, I was utterly unfit to marry a marquess. I was embarrassed that I had let my imagination run away with me. It was a blessing the man could not read my thoughts. "Goodnight, my—"

"Tarquin," he interrupted, coming to a stand. "I didn't mean to frighten you away. But I find I value your opinions, Mrs. Wheeler."

"I cannot think why," I said, without considering.

"If you saw yourself the way I do, you would not question it. I will not do you the dishonor of requesting the use of your given name, but I will no longer abide any my lord from your lips."

"Goodnight." I could not bring myself to call him by his Christian name. He, a future duke. It was absolutely appalling. My mother was likely watching me that very moment and shaking her fist at him for his uncouth behavior.

Although, his motives, I believed, were pure. There was no misunderstanding between us. We had both been very clear from the beginning regarding our feelings, and I believed him when he stated that he simply wanted to be called by his own name. Though it was perhaps an unconventional request, clearly he mourned the loss of his previous life. And if I had read his emotions accurately, he did not have a friend whom he could confide in about this.

I slipped from the room and up the stairs, smiling to myself. I was that friend for him. He might have an unnatural way of acting when separated from the rest of the party, but I found that I enjoyed it very much.

CHAPTER 12

We set out for a walk after breakfast, Mr. Peterson quickly passing out the umbrellas he'd acquired in Gersham.

"The sun is shining, sir," Miss Thornton said, eyeing him with confusion. "But I suppose one never can be too cautious of freckles."

"And one can never be too wary of the possibility of rain," he replied, winking at me.

I ignored him and walked ahead, training my face to the sky to welcome a few freckles, simply to spite Miss Thornton.

Mrs. Haley chose to stay behind with her mother and Mr. Pollard, but the remainder of the party gathered to take a turn about the gardens. And, if Miss Pollard did not object, perhaps the duck pond as well.

Lord Stallsbury offered Miss Thornton his escort and Mr. Peterson followed suit quickly with Miss Pollard. When Mr. Bancroft approached me at the same time as Mr. Thornton, I clasped my hands together and walked between them as we brought up the rear.

"Now tell me how you have been recently," Thornton inquired. "You live with your brother now, I assume."

"Yes, he's taken a house in Linshire. While the society may not be quite as varied as that found in Town, I find that it suits me just fine." I grinned, but Thornton must not have caught on to my joke.

"You were content with Frank in his small country home. I don't see why Linshire should be any different. Though I must admit that I have not visited that part of the country. I am sure, Mrs. Wheeler, that you have the disposition to be quite pleased regardless of your surroundings."

I had to bite my tongue to keep from arguing that point. Was he calling me brainless or merely exceedingly positive? I was only human; I required conversation and companionship as much as any person.

"I find that you lift *my* spirits," Mr. Bancroft said. Clearly, he took Thornton's words to imply acute positivity. "And I believe that you will have the opportunity to get a taste of what Gersham has to offer at church on Sunday, and the ball as well. Mother is endeavoring to fill our ballroom to the brim and has invited a great number of local families."

"That will be delightful, though I must confess I have yet to receive a proper tour of the house. Does it contain a ballroom?"

"You have yet to have a tour? I have been remiss in my duties. The house does contain a ballroom and it is most splendid. See those doors there?" Mr. Bancroft asked, pointing to a row of long rectangular windows flanking a set of doors at the far end of the house. "They lead to the ballroom. Though not as large as one might find in a grander house than ours, it does well enough for our purposes."

"And how fortunate you are to have the ability to open doors right off the ballroom and into the garden," I said. "I find balls in general easily become too hot and stuffy for my taste and are never sufficiently aired by mere windows. Doors leading outside directly from the ballroom indicate superior design."

Mr. Bancroft preened as though he had designed the house himself, and not his ancestors, and I worked to suppress my grin.

"I do love a good ball," Thornton said, clasping his hands behind his back. "Always a decent card game to be had, and a spot of dancing available when one tires of losing."

This was no surprise to me, given how often he took Frank away to lose money at cards. Evidently, neither of them were very successful when it came to *winning*.

We followed the group through the gardens, admiring the shaped hedges and pruned flowers. Circling back around the lawn I discovered that we were approaching the duck pond when I noticed Miss Pollard visibly stiffen before me.

"Any good fishing, Bancroft?" Thornton asked over my head.

"We've got a decent stock of trout. They aren't too eager to bite but you are welcome to it if you'd like to give it a try."

The ducks swam lazily along in the shallows, one meandering about a patch of grass on the bank. Miss Pollard's steps slowed until they were directly before us and I caught her glancing between her escort, Mr. Peterson, and Miss Thornton just ahead of us. If I was not mistaken, she was panicking, and likely hoped to keep her fear of ducks unknown to our present company. Given Mr. Peterson's constant teasing, and Miss Thornton's need to be superior, I found that I did not blame her.

"Mr. Bancroft," I said loudly, clutching his arm, "would you be so kind as to escort me back into the house? I find that the warmth of the sun is giving me a headache and I think it would be best if I returned inside."

"That is likely wise. You would not want to ruin our lovely outing with rain," Mr. Peterson said, clever man that he was.

"Oh, you poor creature!" Miss Pollard gushed, bouncing to

my side at once. "I shall bring you inside immediately. I can see that you are clearly unwell."

Must she go that far? I was doing this to aid her, after all.

"Thank you, Miss Pollard," Mr. Bancroft said chivalrously, "but I do not mind escorting Mrs. Wheeler inside."

"I shall come," she demanded, gripping my arm so tightly I was sure to bruise. "Now let's get you into the house right away, Mrs. Wheeler."

She dragged me away at a decent clip, Mr. Bancroft scurrying to keep up. I did my best to keep my smile to myself and glanced over my shoulder to find the remainder of our party following us at a sedate pace, Miss Thornton once again on Lord Stallsbury's arm, the other two men flanking them.

She had lost no time in putting herself into the marquess's good graces, that was certain. Surely I had no room to complain. At least he had been correct. They would rub along well together. Neither, it seemed, were overly concerned with obtaining a love match, and the connections were sufficient to please both families well enough.

Not that Miss Thornton had much of a family to please, her brother being her guardian and the last remaining member of her immediate family.

I turned my attention to the woman who was now digging her fingers into the flesh of my upper arm.

"Miss Pollard, you may release me now," I whispered, "we are nearly back at the house."

She let go at once and relief instantly swept through my arm.

"I do apologize for keeping you in the sun too long," Mr. Bancroft said, his eyes downcast with sorrow.

"It is not common for me to be bothered by the sun," I explained quickly. "I am sure I shall be fit for company again quite soon."

It would not do to marry a man and have him think I was too weak of constitution to enjoy a hearty walk in the sunlight. It was, in fact, one of my most favorite things to do to occupy my time. While the headache I claimed was not entirely feigned—Miss Thornton's droning was positively weighing on me—claiming it was due to overexposure was certainly false. But I could not feel guilt for the lie when it saved Miss Pollard from extreme distress and subsequent embarrassment.

I thought to ask her the cause of her fear the next time we were alone, for it made little sense to me. Ducks were so small, and quite harmless little creatures. And they were darling, besides.

"I should love to give you a tour of the house when you return from resting," Mr. Bancroft said, leading me to the base of the staircase while Miss Pollard let herself into the drawing room. "Please let me know if you find yourself in need of anything."

He picked up my hand and placed a kiss on the back of my glove. I glanced up as the front door opened and watched the rest of the party filter inside.

"Mrs. Wheeler," Mr. Peterson called from the foyer. "You shall never credit it, but it has begun to rain!"

I chuckled to myself, ignoring his playful grin. The open doorway revealed fine weather, but water drops on Mr. Peterson's umbrella were evidence that he spoke the truth. Though I did not think I would count a small sprinkling of rain that occurred *after* I stepped into the house as evidence of my curse.

Lord Stallsbury released Miss Thornton, watching me with puzzled eyes as I thanked my escort and turned up the stairs. I felt his gaze follow me until I disappeared from his sight, and released the breath I'd been keeping in.

Eager for the rest of the day to pass so that I might have the opportunity to speak privately to the marquess, I found myself too anxious to relax. Pulling the novel from my trunk, I made myself comfortable on the bed and found my place, forcing myself to delve into the story of the young heroine and her high-wayman-turned-earl.

Lord Stallsbury might not be my hero, but he surely played a large role in my ability to find the house party enjoyable. I was sure that he would find Miss Pollard's fear of ducks quite as entertaining as I did—and furthermore, he would be willing to help her out of any future situations in which she would prefer not to inform the rest of the party about her irrational fear.

Sharing the information with Lord Stallsbury would not be breaking the trust of a friend, it would be aiding her in support.

With that neat little line of justification, I nestled into my book, pleased at once to find myself enjoying the story as I'd hoped.

I had fallen asleep during the final chapter of my novel and awoke to Emma laying out an evening gown for dinner. Rubbing my eyes, I pulled myself to sit up and swung my legs over the side of the bed.

"I cannot believe I slept so long." Yawning, I realized that it was, in fact, entirely believable. I had been staying up late every night since my arrival at Bancroft Hill with conversation in the study. It was no wonder that I found myself lethargic and in need of a restoring nap.

"The house here is quite unrivaled, is it not?" I asked, watching Emma put up my hair through the looking glass.

"Yes, ma'am."

I could not tell whether Emma had glanced away due to my question, or if she had simply been focusing on my hair. But a flit of feeling in my gut told me that there was something which she was not sharing.

"Emma, are you well?"

"Of course," she said, her widened eyes finding mine in the mirror.

Clearly I had surprised her with my question. "But the house, it is not to your liking?"

"The house is lovely, ma'am."

I felt as though I was yanking along a particularly stubborn mule. Would she not simply come forth with whatever it was that was bothering her?

I lowered my voice. "Emma, come. Tell me what is bothering you. I can see that something is not right."

Her hands paused, her eyes flicking to mine momentarily before she fixed them securely on my hair. "The house is lovely and I've no qualms with the other servants. 'Tis only that I heard some women talking. I'm sure it's nothing, ma'am, but I can't shake it."

I tried not to stare at her too closely, but my body went still. Something did not feel right.

"I don't make it a habit of listening to conversations," Emma continued. "'Tis only that they were talking about you, ma'am, so I hid behind the door and listened."

I bit my tongue and shoved back the temptation to correct her horrid speech. "What were they saying?"

She paused, her hands lingering over my head. I wanted to turn around and demand that she speak but did not want to frighten her. I could only hope the wait she was forcing me to endure would be far more uncomfortable than the secret she had yet to reveal.

"They were saying you came down in the world and aren't fit to be mistress of Bancroft Hill. That you were only here because you're greedy and feeding on Mr. Bancroft's infatuation."

My hands shook as I lowered them to my lap. "Who said this, Emma?"

She lifted her shoulder. "Don't know, ma'am. I was hiding."

I nodded, my gaze trained forward. I could only guess that

the speaker of such cruel and unkind thoughts was either Miss Thornton, fueled no doubt by her anger over our shared past, or Mrs. Bancroft. The idea that such severe words could come from the woman who was to be my mother-in-law stung. But I could not lay blame without proper knowledge. It would not do to feel a similar dislike for a woman who had not earned my wrath.

When Emma completed my toilette, I closed my eyes and let out a long sigh, breathing out the negativity that itched my body and unsettled my spirit.

Mr. Peterson met me at the base of the stairs, bowing and offering his escort to the drawing room. "I trust you had a pleasant nap? You have missed an eventful day of whist, dear madam," he said. "And I believe the women have prepared a game of charades for us to play this evening."

"Splendid," I said, doing my utmost to appear excited. "I haven't participated in charades in quite a few years. I am likely rusty."

"Nonsense. I am sure it will all come back to you the moment we begin."

We entered the drawing room and a sudden hush fell over the occupants. Mrs. Bancroft stood near the fireplace, cheeks ruddy, chest heaving in indignation.

Mrs. Haley stood beside her, her hands forward in a placating gesture, watching Mr. Bancroft with confusion and anxiety. I admit that my acquaintance with Mr. Bancroft was short in its entirety and I did not know him as well as I would have liked, but it was clear to me that he was angry—no, furious—and I had never before seen such blatant displeasure on his face.

"Mrs. Wheeler!" Mrs. Haley shrieked, her mother and brother turning toward me in accord. Instantaneously the anger dropped from their countenances, Mrs. Bancroft displaying tight irritation, and Mr. Bancroft the very picture of congeniality.

My chest went cold, fear and confusion swirling inside me. I'd had no reason thus far to question the sense of a union between Mr. Bancroft and myself, no need to fear the man I had thought gentle and kind. I had once vowed never to wed a man who did not hold me in as high regard as I did him, and I had thought that Mr. Bancroft was a safe choice. That I hadn't known him capable of such fierce anger before opened the door to the possibility that I might not know his character as well as I thought.

The idea frightened me, exceedingly.

"Do you need to remove yourself for a moment?" Mr. Peterson asked, his voice calm and pacifying. I turned toward his steady gaze and saw at once the facade of teasing lifted and his clear countenance gauging my reaction. Mr. Pollard sat just to our left, his head drooping with the onset of a nap. I truly could not figure out how a man was capable of sleeping so consistently. I merely shook my head and allowed him to lead me toward the window.

"Mr. Peterson?"

"Hmm?" He turned toward me.

"Do you truly believe me cursed?"

He glanced from me to the window streaming with rain. The clouds beyond were thick, the late afternoon sky positively dark. Candlelight reflected on the water drops clinging to the panes, causing the window to glow and us to find our own reflections in the window shrouded by drips and lines of rain. It was mesmerizing and beautiful, and I found my reflective nature enthralled by the image.

"Many people do believe in curses," he said at length. "Have you not found yourself the brunt of nature's joke, with no other recourse but to manage her wrath with humor?"

"I certainly have these last few days."

He chuckled. "Perhaps you needn't allow her to win."

"You mean," I clarified, turning toward the man instead of watching him in the window, "I must choose to not be cursed and then the rain will cease? That sounds fantastical, sir."

"There is a lot of power in the nature of choice, Mrs. Wheeler. You may not be able to control the weather, but you can control a great many things about you if you merely choose to."

I faced the window, uncertain if his meaning held any value, or what had spurred the insightful revelation. It was simple for a man to say that one could choose happiness; he had not been subject to the whim of an angry, distanced husband or a drunk of a brother. But that was in the past; Mr. Bancroft was my future.

"What a solemn gathering," Miss Thornton observed, sweeping into the room and delicately lowering herself into the chair nearest Mrs. Bancroft. "By my word, I do believe that we need a little something to raise our spirits, ma'am."

Mrs. Bancroft murmured something I could not hear, to which Miss Thornton chuckled. "When I was last in London there was a hostess quite inept at fostering interesting gatherings. At one such dinner my dear brother took it upon himself to assist the family, procuring a fine game of charades that fairly put everyone into a good humor."

"If you believe charades to be the fix for a dull party, what does that have to say for our plans this evening?" Mr. Peterson asked, his teasing nature restored.

"That I quite enjoy the game," Miss Thornton responded, her hands primly folded and a dainty smile touching her lips. Her intelligent gaze sought mine and I held it. Was she the woman who spoke ill of me earlier? I would not put it past her. In truth, the woman was a puzzle. I felt such dislike in her gaze, but there was little in her actions to reinforce the feelings.

Lord Stallsbury entered the room, Miss Pollard shortly behind him. He greeted the women before strolling languidly toward Mr. Peterson and me.

"Did you enjoy your letter?" he asked, coming to rest his dark gaze on me.

"I know not to what you refer, my lord."

A brief flick of emotion passed through his eyes. "There was a letter delivered earlier, while you were indisposed. I supposed it was brought to you by your maid."

I shook my head, anxiety beginning to swirl within me. It had not been long enough for Charlotte to receive my letter and send a reply. Could she have horrible news that could not wait? "My maid said nothing."

"I wouldn't refine too much on it," Mr. Peterson said.

The butler came to the door to announce dinner and we filed into the room, taking our seats while Miss Thornton chatted loudly with Mrs. Bancroft and Lord Stallsbury at the other end of the table. Her voice grew more shrill the longer I was forced to endure it. My teeth ground together in irritation, my fork grasped far too firmly in my hand.

"It is my belief," I could hear her say, "that anyone might be put into a good humor with small and simple actions. It is not necessary to always procure large gestures to obtain affection, but the small things add up to create joy."

"Do you agree, Mrs. Wheeler?"

I jumped, Mr. Bancroft's voice soft but loud in my ear when I was straining to eavesdrop on Miss Thornton. His eyes were earnest, his head tilted in concern.

"You seem to be focusing so keenly," he continued, "I assumed you had an opinion on the matter."

I took a bite, chewing my food slowly to allow myself the time to gather my thoughts. How was I to tell him that the woman simply didn't seem as though she liked me, and as a result I was not very fond of her? It would not paint me in the best light. Instead, I said, "I believe any healthy relationship might be strengthened by small acts of kindness, naturally. I do not think large gestures are entirely necessary, but perhaps are valuable to boost one's esteem. In that, it may depend on the nature and strength of the relationship to begin with."

"Do you find yourself in need of large gestures to aid affection?" he questioned.

Lowering my fork, I searched Mr. Bancroft's gentle, pleasant face. Yet my mind continually jumped back to the image of him facing his mother, livid. I could not remove from my thoughts his face, mottled with rage, altering within a moment to calm congeniality.

Was it simply the nature of men to be quick to anger? It was a distinct possibility that I had created an image of the perfect gentleman and assigned it to Mr. Bancroft. It was unfair of me to hold him to such standards when the rest of humanity was allowed grace.

Lowering my lashes, I cast my eyes downward. "I am not sure," I began, answering his question. "I suppose it would depend on the gesture. I am not so frivolous, I would like to think, as to require great gestures of affection. But what woman would deny the basic kindnesses that build and create love? A small bouquet or handwritten poem do not cause the giver much hardship, but cause them to grow in the woman's esteem greatly, do they not?"

His thick eyebrows pulled together in consideration, a sandy brown curl flopping forward as he nodded his head. "I suppose I had not considered it that way."

"Do not refine upon it too much, Mr. Bancroft. I am not so shallow as to hinge my affections upon small gifts or gestures."

He turned an endearing smile upon me. "No, my dear, I should say that you are not."

Returning to my meal, I glanced down the table and watched Miss Thornton entertain Lord Stallsbury with the greatest ease. She was perfect for the role of his future duchess, and I could see that he was busy making the same conclusion for himself.

CHAPTER 13

Miss Pollard stood before the grouping of chairs, doing her utmost to imitate what I believed was a rabbit.

"A bird? A duck?" Mr. Peterson questioned, running a hand through his hair. "I cannot tell while you flap and jump at the same time, Miss Pollard, if you are intending to fly or leap."

Chuckles broke out among the audience and poor Miss Pollard's face turned scarlet.

"I believe I warned you all that this game was not my forte," she said crisply.

"You are doing well, my dear," Mrs. Bancroft said, her voice low and soothing. "Now what were you? A sparrow?"

"I was attempting to be a fox."

"Yes, of course," Mr. Peterson said, his grin stretching dangerously across his face. "Naturally, that was meant to be a fox."

"You may take a turn next, sir, so that you might see how very difficult playacting can be."

Mr. Peterson dutifully stood. He pulled a slip of paper from the bowl and considered it a moment before folding and tucking it into his waistcoat pocket.

Immediately he began squatting as though he sat upon something, holding one arm forward as another raised in imitation of a whip. He galloped about the stage area until Thornton cried, "Clearly you are riding a horse."

Mr. Peterson quit at once, languidly resuming his seat with a smug smile playing on his lips. Miss Pollard frowned.

"Mrs. Wheeler, would you like to go next?" Miss Thornton asked, as though she was the hostess of the party. I glanced to Mrs. Bancroft—the *actual* hostess—but she did not seem the least bothered by the control Miss Thornton took. I gave the younger woman a tight smile and drew a paper from the bowl.

Fishing.

Well, that was simple enough. I had never fished before, myself, but I had watched my brother a time or two and I knew the basic actions well enough. I took myself to the center of the stage and turned to the side, holding an invisible fishing pole. It was more difficult than I imagined, for there was no way to explain that the item I held was long and thin.

Casting back, I let the line fly forward with a smooth motion in my arm.

"Throwing rocks!" Miss Pollard guessed.

I shook my head, casting the pole again.

"Throwing an arrow?" she guessed again.

As though that made any sense. I shook my head again as she screwed up her face in thought. Why was no one else guessing? Surely the men knew of what I was physically describing for they planned to take part in the activity themselves the very next day.

I cast my line once again and Lord Stallsbury said, "You are fishing."

I turned my smile on him, grateful to not be left upon the

stage for a great length of time casting pretend lines into an invisible pond. "Well done, my lord!"

Resuming my seat, Lord Stallsbury replaced me on the stage. He pulled a paper from the bowl and a smile tipped his lips before he looked directly at me. Had he gotten my paper? My contribution had been something of a joke, realizing that the likelihood of him choosing it was slim.

He stood before us, smiling at me before forcing his face into a straight expression. Standing still, he held his hands before him in prayer. That was odd; perhaps he did not have my slip of paper after all. He quickly moved over two paces and held out a hand expectantly, then mimed putting a ring onto an invisible hand. Moving back to the first position, he held his hands in prayer again and then looked at us expectantly.

Clearly, charades was not a talent for Lord Stallsbury. He *did* have my paper, I could see it now. But everyone else in the room remained unaware of what he could possibly be showing us. He must have gauged the confusion in the room for he sighed and crossed toward me, offering me his hand.

I placed my own inside his and he led me to the stage. It was my fault that he chose to use me as a prop, for he must have known that I wrote the difficult prompt. Nevertheless, using another person was against the rules, surely. I glanced about the audience but they either did not see anything wrong with it or they chose to let it slide. He was a marquess, after all.

He stood beside me, taking my hand in his own and mimicked sliding a ring onto my finger. I glanced up into his dark brown eyes and my heart pounded against my breastbone. Flashbacks to my first marriage in Aunt Mary's small church flooded my memory, but were swiftly squashed by the endearing smile on Lord Stallsbury's face.

"Wedding! It is a wedding," Mrs. Haley shouted, clapping for herself.

He tore his gaze from my face and bowed to the audience,

gesturing toward me until I curtsied. "The card read marriage," he said, "but I believe wedding is close enough."

I chuckled to relieve the tension in my shoulders and moved to resume my seat. Miss Thornton's stormy gaze was not lost on me, and neither was Mr. Bancroft's.

Mrs. Haley took her place on the stage and the game continued as though nothing had happened. Which was true. Nothing *had* happened. I was caught up in the moment of play-acting a marriage and it brought both pleasant and unpleasant feelings to the forefront of my thoughts. I was fortunate to avoid a repeat performance and when it was time to leave the gentlemen and prepare for bed, I was shocked to find Miss Thornton immediately on my arm, clutching me as we made our exit.

"You did splendidly in there, Mrs. Wheeler. Absolutely delightful."

This she said about my pretend fishing.

"Thank you, Miss Thornton. It was a pleasant way to pass the evening."

"Yes, quite." She watched me a moment as we stood outside my bedchamber. "Goodnight, Mrs. Wheeler."

"Goodnight, Miss Thornton."

I escaped into my bedroom, allowing Emma to undress me and help me into my night rail. I wanted to believe Miss Thornton was genuine in her praises, but my gut would not allow it. There was something off about the woman, but I could not put my finger on what it was.

"Did a letter come for me today while I was asleep?" I asked Emma.

"Not that I know of, but I can ask."

I agreed and she left to inquire after the post.

I sat on the edge of my bed watching the candle flicker on the table beside me. I had made the decision earlier that there would be no need for a meeting this evening with the marquess as I had one chapter remaining in my book and surely Lord Stallsbury had nothing he needed to discuss. I was no expert on relationships, clearly, but he seemed to be progressing well with Miss Thornton.

I was progressing rapidly with Mr. Bancroft, myself, though the idea frightened me now. I waited for Emma to return, my gaze locked on the flickering flame and the shadow it cast on the wall.

"You were correct," Emma said, coming into the room. "This arrived earlier." She held forth a folded, sealed letter and I took it, waiting for her to take my gown and leave me for the night.

As soon as the door closed behind my maid, I slid the seal open and unfolded Charlotte's letter. I devoured the words, fear and anticipation pulling me forward until I read the sentences I most feared.

There was trouble.

I shut my eyes, dropping the letter on my lap. How was I to help Charlotte when I was so far away? Refusing to cry, I crossed to the window and then back. Pacing, I shook my arms out to relieve built up pressure and considered Charlotte's words. She was not in immediate peril. That was the first point to her benefit.

The second, that Miss Hurst was, herself, quite capable of handling the situation. Charlotte was in good hands.

I picked up the letter once more and read through it, past the pleasantries and update on the superb stables at Corden Hall— Mr. Bryce was a horse breeder and Charlotte was bound to be in heaven among his superior steeds—and to her brief mention of the chatter she had heard in Linshire: Noah was drinking himself to sleep at the inn now, instead of at home. Remarks had been made in Charlotte's presence that were not kind, and Mr. Bryce, Miss Hurst's betrothed, was called upon to check on the nature of Noah's well-being.

Of course, Mr. Bryce had not been permitted inside the

house, but was able to see well enough that our brother was alive, though unfit for company. It was the precise description I could have given over the course of the last few years.

The only difference was that until now, Noah had not created too large a spectacle of himself. Our cottage was well built, but bare. On the outside, no one had cause to assume our poverty. We had done a decent job, I hoped, of convincing the people in town that we were not excessively poor and our brother was merely antisocial, not a drunk. He was quickly undoing all of my hard work.

What would Charlotte do when Noah made his situation clear to the people in town? Her reputation would not survive it, surely.

To move my mind from the trouble at home, I picked up my book, sitting before the fire for better light.

Three quarters of an hour later, I had made no progress beyond the first paragraph, several lines of which I had read repeatedly. My poor heroine was about to receive her hero and their happily ever after and I could not force myself to focus enough on the pages to see them to completion. I dropped the book on the floor, holding my face in my hands.

There was nothing for it, I needed to go down to him.

I pulled on slippers and my thick dressing gown, buttoning it at the neck and tying the sash tightly around my waist. I was fully covered, if not completely clothed, and I would go to the library first to choose a novel in the event that I was caught.

I paced the room another quarter of an hour to be sure that the way would be clear before I poked my head out the door. The house was dark. None of the guest bedrooms on this floor had the least bit of light spilling under their doorways. I crept to the stairs and down to the proper hallway, my heart racing at the faint glow of light under the study door.

No sooner had I opened the door to the library than I realized my mistake. Two voices, both male, were murmuring softly near the low burning fire.

"Oh!" I said, despite myself. To slip away quietly would have been significantly better, but now I had outed myself and Mr. Bancroft and Thornton both turned in unison, surprised.

"Mrs. Wheeler, are you well?" Mr. Bancroft inquired, jumping to his feet.

I nodded. "I was merely searching out a novel. I find I cannot fall asleep."

His face fell. "Is your bedchamber uncomfortable? Is the bed not to your liking? Or do you have a noise keeping you awake?"

His concern was nearly suffocating. "No, no. Nothing of the sort. I simply have not grown used to the bedchamber yet, and I enjoy reading in the evenings."

He nodded as though my explanation was reasonable.

"I find I must scurry back to my room. I would not care to be caught out."

Thornton stood. "Shall I escort you?"

"No," I said, backing out the door. "This is not quite appropriate, sir. Just pretend you never saw me and I will take better care to explore the library in the daylight hours."

I shut the door behind me with enough force that the men would heed my wishes, I hoped. I had barely managed a glimpse of the bookcases, but I had to admit that Mr. Bancroft was correct in his original description, the library looked positively glorious and I could not wait to return the following morning for a thorough evaluation.

"What are you doing out here?"

I jumped at Lord Stallsbury's voice. Though, gratefully, I didn't squeal. Squinting my eyes, I could barely make out his outline in the opposite doorway. He had been so sly that I hadn't even noticed the door open.

"I went into the library for a book," I whispered. "And discovered Mr. Bancroft and Thornton inside."

He looked as serious as he sounded. "You must return to your room at once."

Irritation made its unpleasant way through me. "That is what I intended to do, my lord."

He nodded, his shadowed face an image of tight aggravation. "Very good. Goodnight then."

I turned away without responding. Climbing the stairs, I felt very much the fool. Lord Stallsbury stood in the hallway and watched me go, and I caught his gaze over my shoulder just before I moved out of sight. Perhaps that was the end of our midnight chats.

I would have to find a way to be satisfied with that.

CHAPTER 14

Mrs. Bancroft stood in the hallway leading into the breakfast room as though waiting for something. Or, perhaps it was *someone*.

I watched her as I descended the staircase. Her eyes hardened as they fell upon me and I smiled. "Good morning, Mrs. Bancroft."

"Would you be so kind as to accompany me to the drawing room for a spell?" she said, her words short and crisp like tin soldiers. "I would like to discuss something with you."

Unease at once filled my person and I nodded, following her to the drawing room. She closed the door behind me with a soft click and spun to face me, her hands clasped tightly.

"You will be seated."

I obeyed.

"Now, we shall not beat about the bush," she said, seating herself opposite me. "You know that my son invited you here because he was considering you for his wife."

Was? I nodded, though I felt faintly positive she did not require a response.

"And I am sure you are aware that I was never fond of the match to begin with."

Where could she possibly be going with this?

She continued, "While I will not pretend that my mind is changed, I see that William has the ability to decide for himself who he will marry. That being said, whomever he takes to wife will have to reside in Bancroft Hill with me, and I can pleasantly say I am healthy and robust, and I shall not be going anywhere anytime soon. You may choose to go against my wishes and marry my son, but I will have you know that regardless of what you do or say I will *never* support your union and I will do everything in my power to make your existence here at Bancroft Hill an unpleasurable one. It is my duty to protect my family, and I do not want my son marrying into such disgrace."

She stood to go, her words delivered and wrapping me in an uncomfortable haze. Disgrace? What did she know about me?

Turning at the door, she speared me with a glare. "Do not repeat this to a soul, or I shall be happy to tell the party that your drunk of a brother is at fault for not only his own poor existence, but your parents' deaths, as well."

I felt as though the carpet was ripped from beneath me. "That is untrue."

Her eyebrow lifted. "Ask him, then, if you do not believe me. Your brother was driving the carriage during the accident. He said himself that he is lucky to be alive."

"When have you spoken to him?" I asked, my eyebrows drawn together. "How do you know this?"

Her smug lips turned sour. "It is true, and if you do not refuse my son then the whole of London Society shall be reminded of it. Do not tempt me, child, for I should not mind ruining you."

She spun away, the derision dripping from her tone spearing me like a hundred tiny barbs.

The door snapped closed behind her, causing me to flinch.

She could not have meant that, surely. Noah suffered from a dependence on drink, but that had nothing to do with the death of my parents. He could not have been driving, for he was not even with them at the time.

No one would believe her lies, would they?

My appetite gone, I sat on the sofa staring mindlessly out the bright window. The sun shone with nary a cloud to be seen across the blue sky. The recent rain and bright light made the grass brighter. It was an inviting scene when faced with the stuffy drawing room and the lingering effects of Mrs. Bancroft's verbal assault.

Mrs. Haley let herself into the drawing room and pulled up short. "Mrs. Wheeler, I was unaware that you were in here. The men have gone fishing so Miss Pollard and I were getting up a group to walk to the wood. Would you like to accompany us?"

I watched her kind, rounded eyes and found them void of malice. While her mother clearly did not care for my presence, I didn't think Mrs. Haley shared the same ill feelings. I stood, nodding. I would not tuck tail and run home so easily. Not before I had time to consider my options. "I would love to come. Allow me to fetch my bonnet first."

"Of course."

I made my way upstairs, Mrs. Bancroft's threats repeating over and over again in my mind. She might not have any say on who her son chose to marry, but she had a lot of say on whether I could lead a happy existence in this home. I glanced about me, imagining myself as the mistress of Bancroft Hill.

While I knew myself capable of running a large house, I didn't quite know how I felt about attempting to do so while the previous mistress stood by and sabotaged my every move. Even if I had Mr. Bancroft's sole support, would it be worth it?

I hardly knew. But Charlotte's letter sat in my trunk reminding me of my reasons for being here. The house party was not over yet and I had plenty of time to reach a decision. Nothing needed to be settled today.

"Mother has had the most bizarre notion to hold a large dinner party in a few days' time," Mrs. Haley said as we crossed the lawn. Miss Thornton and Miss Pollard walked beside us and I was proud of myself for not stumbling on the pronouncement. I could not fathom how a dinner party might be connected to Mrs. Bancroft's threat, but something within me felt strongly that it was, and I was not eager to discover how.

"Will she be able to fill her table with such little notice?" Miss Thornton asked, her tone disbelieving.

"Certainly," Mrs. Haley replied at once. "You must realize that we are the largest house in the parish. Mother never struggles to fill her table."

"With *quality*, though?" Miss Thornton argued.

Mrs. Haley paused, looking a little piqued. "Yes, of course."

"Tell me about London, Miss Thornton," I said, hoping to encourage her to speak about herself, thus relieving Mrs. Haley. "I have not been in years."

"I've only just completed a Season and it was just as enjoyable as always," she said. "The endless balls and parties are an absolute dream, of course."

Miss Pollard sighed. "How glorious. I cannot wait until I may experience the London Season. I've been to London, but never the *ton* parties. I am afraid my father will never take me, so I must rely on a husband. Though, perhaps it is best to find a husband *during* the Season, isn't it?"

I had only seen Mr. Pollard awake a handful of times, and most of those were during mealtimes. I could see how the idea of the Season might put him off.

"You will likely enjoy it more after you wed," Mrs. Haley said. "I surely did once the pressure to marry was relieved."

Nodding sagely, Miss Thornton added, "It's true. It is not for the weak of heart. You must be voracious if you plan to snag a husband. The good ones are always taken quickly."

"I had thought at one point that I wouldn't need to put any effort into obtaining a husband," Miss Pollard lamented. "But of course, that is no longer the case."

All three of the women's heads swiveled my direction and I felt my cheeks warm.

Miss Pollard seemed to realize her mistake and blushed accordingly. At least I could reasonably claim that I did not intend on stealing the man she had her eye on, for I had not even known of her existence before arriving at Bancroft Hill. And in my defense, he did not seem the least interested in her.

Miss Thornton, of course, was a different story altogether. Frank had told me of his fleeting affection for her in his youth. He also had explained that he was long past the infatuation and I needn't fear any lingering feelings. Miss Thornton, on the other hand, seemed to still harbor feelings aplenty. Though my marriage had occurred three and a half years ago, Miss Thornton did not seem the least inclined to forgive or forget.

Some people, it seemed, never were.

"My brother has always cared for you as something of a sister," Mrs. Haley said to Miss Pollard. "He has always looked after you, of course. He is such a generous man."

I did my best to mask my surprise. Mrs. Haley's diplomatic response was an explanation I'd yet to hear. Though I had to admit, it is precisely what I had assumed to be the case.

We approached the edge of the wood. The servants had come ahead of us and set a table under the shade with an array of picnic items. Cold meats, cheese and fruit were all spread on a tray with cool lemonade prepared in cups.

I had to smile to myself. Hadn't Mr. Bancroft mentioned that the only way to entice his sister on a walk was to place a picnic at the end of it? She helped herself to a chair immediately and sipped at her lemonade.

"My, but this sun has surely wiped the energy right out of me," she said, sighing. "I'm utterly exhausted."

"How thoughtful of you to request a picnic," Miss Pollard said. "I vow, you think of everything."

"One must when one's husband hopes to become a member of parliament," Mrs. Haley said over the rim of her glass of lemonade. "It is just as much up to me as it is to him to provide the proper social connections."

Miss Pollard sighed. "How lovely to be so needed."

I sat in the shade, glancing out over the lawn and the majestic house. The pond to the far side completed the picturesque view and the men fishing on the opposite bank added a nice touch.

"Do the ducks always stay right near the pond?" Miss Pollard asked, her voice rising in pitch.

I bit my tongue to keep from laughing. A particularly large duck had waddled from the water and some distance up the bank. It was as if the little fowl knew of Miss Pollard's fear and chose to set her on edge with his slow progression toward us.

Mrs. Haley's eyebrows scrunched together over the rim of her teacup as she took a sip. "Usually, yes, but that one seems adventurous today."

The resulting giggle Miss Pollard delivered was shrill and nervous. I could not blame her, for the duck slowly continued toward us. We watched it meander for some time before it had the grace to turn away and put more distance between us.

"Mrs. Wheeler," Miss Thornton said, her lips curved into a catlike grin, "you are quiet today. Is there something plaguing your mind?"

Aside from the curse that had followed me since London, a drunk brother, a sister in need of care, a potential mother-in-law who despised me, and a life-altering decision to make over the course of the next week? No, nothing at all.

I tried to mimic her smile as best I could. "Everything is positively ordinary."

"Indeed."

We all raised our glasses in accord and sipped the bitter liquid.

CHAPTER 15

"Meet me tonight?"

I jumped back against the wall. Lord Stallsbury had stepped from behind the staircase suddenly and my hand flew up to calm my beating heart. "My lord, you frightened me something fierce. You really must quit doing that."

His eyes beseeched me.

"I cannot make any promises," I whispered. "The last time we were nearly caught."

He stepped closer. "But I find myself in a dilemma and I would appreciate your advice."

I could not help but stand a little straighter following that pronouncement. "Then can we not do something more respectable to earn us a bit of privacy? We could ride," I offered, "or take a stroll about the gardens?"

"It is not the same and you well know it."

I did know it, in fact. But I found that I liked knowing that he shared the feeling very much. The midnight meetings had an aura of danger to them; they were forbidden, yet I felt that we were untouchable. It was an hour between the day and the night that we could discuss whatever we wished without fear of recourse or retribution.

Unless we were caught, of course. In which we would have no choice but to marry or be ruined.

I swallowed. My family could not possibly weather any more scandal. "I just do not see how it can be done."

"Leave the men to me," he implored. He'd yet to so much as smile and the determination in his eyes was unnerving. "But promise me you'll come."

Caught in his gaze, earnest and unrelenting, I agreed. His returning smile was wide, causing me to miss a step and stumble forward. I righted myself and continued down the hallway, pretending as though I hadn't just nearly tripped in the presence of a marquess.

His chuckle reached me nonetheless and I could not hide my grin as I let myself into the drawing room.

"There you are, Mrs. Wheeler. What think you of having that tour of the house now?" Mr. Bancroft asked, watching me expectantly. Did he truly think a tour would be useful now? I had been in his home as a guest for over a week and knew the house quite well. I had yet to explore the library or the ballroom, and I was sure there were a handful of other rooms I was unaware of, but I could see the man's eagerness to spend time with me and understood that it was a necessary aspect of courting.

With less than a fortnight remaining, I had little time to secure my position within the home if that was still the desired outcome.

I glanced beyond him and found his mother's shrewd gaze locked on me. Swallowing, I nodded slowly. I could not give in to her ridiculous demands. "I should love that, Mr. Bancroft."

"Would anyone else care to join us?"

Miss Pollard stood. An odd choice for a chaperone, but I supposed she was better than none. "I would love to. I haven't explored the house in an age. Mr. Peterson, Mr. Thornton? Have you both seen the house?"

They watched her as if they were deer staring into a rifle. Mr. Peterson finally stood, sacrificing himself for the greater good. "I should love to accompany you, Miss Pollard."

We set out, my hand upon Mr. Bancroft's arm as he led us down a hallway I knew well—while I was in the dark, at least. Now the sunlight lit the space and transformed it into a completely different place.

"That door leads to my study," Mr. Bancroft explained, "though I'm never in there much. Positively boring room if you ask me. My father spent a good deal of time in there but I don't find myself in need of it often."

We turned for the library, and I was at once awed by the exquisite bookcases built into three of the four walls, the fourth was covered almost entirely in windows. A prime source of light, indeed. Clearly whoever designed this room had a penchant for reading and an understanding of the basic necessities. A good book, comfortable chair, and enough light to see; all of which could be found in abundance in this room.

"It is glorious," I said reverently.

"Indeed," Miss Pollard said, "if you enjoy reading."

"Our Mrs. Wheeler has already admitted to a love for reading," Lord Stallsbury said. I turned to find him framed by the doorway, his knowing smile touching me briefly before turning his attention to our host. "Bancroft, may I borrow a mare to take Miss Thornton for a ride?"

"Absolutely," he replied immediately. "My horses are at your disposal. In fact, that is a grand concept. Shall we postpone this tour for another day?"

"I do not think Lord Stallsbury would appreciate us encroaching upon his time," I said, doing my utmost to sound diplomatic.

Mr. Bancroft nodded, a knowing gleam in his eye. "Ahh, yes."

Lord Stallsbury nodded once and left.

"Perhaps we may plan a ride for tomorrow," Miss Pollard offered. "I should enjoy it very much."

"Perhaps. Would you like to see the ballroom?" Mr. Bancroft asked me.

I tried to deliver a grin worthy of his enthusiasm. "Yes, please."

He led us to the ballroom and opened the door with a flourish. We spread out about the room. A dusty chandelier hung from the ceiling, casting its shadow over floorboards worn from years of country dances.

"Shall we test it?" Mr. Peterson asked. He came before me and bowed as though I was a duchess. "A dance, if you please?"

I could not help but chuckle. Dipping into an equally low curtsy, I placed my hand in his. I noticed Mr. Bancroft and Miss Pollard join us on the opposite side of the room and I began to hum a waltz. We promenaded about the room and began the dance. It was a little simpler with only two couples but we managed well enough, making our own adjustments when necessary.

"I believe this room is quite prepared for dancers," Mr. Peterson said, bowing. "And what superb music, Mrs. Wheeler."

"My humming?" I laughed. "You are quite easy to please."

He delivered a rakish grin. "Never say that I didn't pay you compliments, ma'am."

"Of course not," I agreed. "You merely intersperse them between liberal reminders of my curse."

He boomed with laughter, and Mr. Bancroft did not look pleased.

"Shall we continue with our tour?" Miss Pollard asked sweetly. She grasped Mr. Peterson's arm, grinning at me as they passed us. Mr. Bancroft looked bothered; I tried to smile my reassurance but he seemed disinclined to accept it.

"Must you flirt with him like that?" he whispered.

I flinched. His voice had carried and I was sure that while the other couple pretended not to have heard, they most certainly must have.

"He is simply teasing, Mr. Bancroft."

"I can't like it," he growled. His demeanor surly, he led us about the house with clipped descriptions and a lot of silence until the irritation seemed to wear off. By the time we walked through the portrait gallery and upper bedrooms, we were hearing the history of the building and the Bancroft family line.

"You have had quite a few murders in your family, Bancroft," Mr. Peterson said, impressed or disturbed, I couldn't quite tell. "I hadn't any idea."

"Yes," he answered, staring bleakly at a frilly portrait of his great grandfather. "It is not a topic Mother tolerates. We do our best not to discuss it."

"You realize it is through no fault of your own," I said, prior to considering my comment. Of course his family would wish to hide the dark spot upon their history, but I did not want Mr. Bancroft to view it a detriment to his character. He could not have helped what happened to his ancestors.

"Of course," he answered, smiling brightly. "Shall I show you the back gardens now? I believe we've completed our tour of the house."

"That would be lovely." We had seen the back gardens already a few times, but he was clearly uncomfortable and needed an excuse to lead us away from the portrait gallery of sandy, curly-haired Bancrofts with square jaws. The likeness to himself was perhaps jarring.

Mr. Bancroft managed to fully reinstate his pleasant mood and we walked among the perfectly trimmed hedges discussing our favorite pastimes.

"The library is to your satisfaction?" he asked. "You spend a good deal of time reading, I assume?"

Nodding, I halted near a hedge, skimming my hand over the

top of the stiff leaves. How were they able to trim them so immaculately? I was quite impressed by the precision. "I once did," I explained. "In recent years I haven't had quite the same amount of time to donate to the amusement of reading, but I hope to change that in the future. Life simply isn't as agreeable without books in it."

"I shall leave that to you, my dear. I find I cannot quite settle my thoughts long enough to focus on an entire text."

It was on the tip of my tongue to comment on which preference I hoped our children would inherit when I clamped my lips together. Thank heavens. That was a near miss.

"Mrs. Wheeler," Miss Pollard called from the other side of the garden. "I just had a marvelous idea! We shall have another archery tournament. What do you think? We never finished the last one due to the rain, and now it shall be even more enjoyable with added company."

"That would be pleasant." And give me the opportunity to redeem myself after my last display.

Mr. Bancroft said, "Monday, perhaps? I shall organize it right away."

Which, he did. Left on my own, I circled the garden once more, giving Mr. Peterson and Miss Pollard privacy to carry on their conversation. The man did not seem inclined to need it, but the woman did. I had already stolen one suitor from her, I was not about to do anything to jeopardize another.

Slipping back inside the house, I snuck up to my bedroom and closed the door, locking it tightly behind me. After checking to ensure that I was very much alone, I slumped onto the edge of my bed, dropped my face into my hands, and sighed.

While things were progressing at an exceptional rate with Mr. Bancroft, the conversation with his mother refused to leave the forefront of my thoughts. What had seemed so ludicrous initially, now held merit.

Noah was a drunk; there was no denying it. Yet, the chance that he could have been responsible in some form for my parents' deaths was as improbable as it was possible. And that terrified me immensely.

CHAPTER 16

The sun streamed through the open bed curtains, waking me early. I sucked in a shallow breath and sat up directly, my ribs uncomfortable from the corset. Oh dear, I'd fallen asleep above my coverlet waiting for an appropriately late hour to take myself down to the study.

"Emma," I gasped when she came in with a prepared gown for church. "Please loosen my stays, I cannot breathe."

"You've slept in them, ma'am?" She dropped the gown on the edge of my bed and rushed to my side. "'Tis sorry, I am. I thought you were going to ring for me when you were ready for bed."

That had been my excuse, hadn't it?

She came behind me, unlacing yesterday's gown and helping me into a new one. She left the back open while she put up my hair, and I breathed deeply while I was able. I could not continue to sleep in my stays. The discomfort was acute and I felt it with every stretch of my lungs.

I first saw Lord Stallsbury just before I entered the carriage for church, his dark gaze piercing me with blame as he sat high atop his glorious horse. I lifted my eyebrows in response. Could he honestly hold me to the midnight meetings so pointedly? Chagrined, I claimed a seat beside Mrs. Haley, watching the men through the window.

Lord Stallsbury did not seem overly bothered, smiling cheerfully with Mr. Peterson. Surely he would understand; I only needed a chance to explain. He *would* understand and would likely encourage me to try again. I felt fairly certain Lord Stallsbury took pleasure in the secret we had between us.

"Your little parish is quite lovely, ma'am," Miss Pollard said, as we pulled out of the drive. "It has been so long since we've come that I quite forgot how beautiful these country lanes are."

"They remind me of home," Miss Thornton said. "Though I've spent so long in London I am not quite sure I am able to call Kent home any longer."

"You may," Mrs. Haley said with authority. "Your heart will always yearn for the place where you spent your tender years. 'Twas then you did not feel the responsibilities of adulthood."

Miss Pollard laughed with discomfort, glancing between her father and Mrs. Bancroft. "You make adulthood sound so bleak."

Mrs. Haley's bright smile belied her words. "Of course not. I am only reflecting on the differences. I had not realized as a child how very blessed and naive I was at the time."

Miss Thornton grinned. "Every child dreams of adulthood, and every adult laments for simpler times. Is it not so?"

"Indeed, it is," Mrs. Haley agreed.

The carriage quieted. I would not answer aloud, but it was a true statement in my experience. I would give almost anything I owned to return to the simpler life before Noah had discovered his affinity for drink and my parents had died in the wretched carriage accident.

But if I did, would I have acted differently as I grew through those experiences? Likely not. Without the experience from which to glean wisdom, nothing could be altered.

I glanced up to find Mrs. Bancroft's pinched face watching

me, and immediately shifted my gaze to the window. She was sour and unfriendly, masking her displeasure less and less with each passing day.

I watched through the window as trees and hills passed by. Lord Stallsbury rode into view and I watched him unabashedly for a stretch. He sat tall and refined, very much like a man who knew his place in the world and was quite unashamed of it. Though his title came to him later, it was evident that he wore it well, in a gracious way, not as highhanded as many men of half his rank.

We rolled to a stop before the church yard and Mr. Bancroft stood by as the step was let down and each of the women—and Mr. Pollard—were handed out of the carriage. Mr. Bancroft escorted me into the church building. When we passed the marquess, his gaze prickled the back of my neck.

It was difficult to focus in church. The time passed horridly slowly and I was not afforded the opportunity to speak to Lord Stallsbury until long after we arrived home again.

Following dinner, the women gathered to letter invitations to the dinner party Mrs. Bancroft had decided quite belatedly to hold. The men joined us some time later and I did my utmost to ignore Lord Stallsbury's pointed looks and masked inquiries.

He sat idly by, discussing the superior merits of the Bancroft's fine feather mattresses with anyone pleased to listen. "Who could possibly avoid falling promptly asleep when faced with such superior comfort?" he said, shooting me a knowing look.

That brought Mr. Bancroft's gaze my direction, and he studied me, a confused look on his face. He was likely considering my claim to sleeplessness; I promptly dipped my pen and wrote another invitation.

Lord Stallsbury then orchestrated a conversation on the advantages of reading by candlelight as opposed to daylight, consequently sparking a debate about the health of one's eyes when excessive reading occurs—regardless of the source of light. I received many looks then, as well. It appeared I had garnered something of a reputation as a bluestocking.

Finally, he touched on the consideration due one's closest friends, questioning the group at large on how he should manage someone who made promises they did not keep. "I simply cannot find it within my heart to let them go," he said. "Particularly when they contribute something of value which I have grown accustomed to."

I could not help grinning down at my invitations by the end of his monologue.

Miss Thornton commanded the room, taking it upon herself to explain the proper method for disposing of relationships which did not uphold their end of an arrangement.

Her voice grew authoritative. "If they are your inferior then you must cut them right away. You need not even bother with polite conversation if they are to utterly disregard you so disrespectfully." Spearing Lord Stallsbury with a look, she said, "I cannot understand why anyone would break a promise to you, my lord. If the person you speak of is a woman, her actions are even more appalling."

That was certainly brazen of her.

A slow smile formed on his lips, stretching wide before he dipped his head in acknowledgement and then swung his smug gaze toward me. I wanted to scoff at the theatrical nature of his display but I could only applaud—though not literally, of course —for it was quite a performance. One would almost believe he had deeply missed our time together.

"Mrs. Wheeler," he said, surprising me. He hadn't spoken directly to me nearly all day, and I was quite taken aback when he did. Our relationship did not seem real, but rather a fantastical dream that only occurred when no one else was around to confirm its existence.

"Yes?"

"You are quite prepared to show us your superior skill at archery tomorrow, I presume? Our last tournament was abysmally cut short."

There was challenge in his gaze and a set to his jaw that I mirrored. "Of course. If I do not let go of the arrow prematurely, of course."

My comment earned a round of light laughter from about the room before Miss Thornton took the opportunity to explain how she had only recently learned the proper technique to shoot an arrow and she absolutely could not wait to try once again. Given her excessive explanations on her lack of experience, I fully expected her to do very well.

The hour grew late and I was exceedingly tired. I stood to excuse myself from the group and Mrs. Haley followed suit. My attention was drawn to Lord Stallsbury and I found his direct gaze powerful. He did not need to speak to communicate to me that he expected me in the study that evening, and he would not let it slide a second night in a row.

I did nothing to indicate that I understood the message, but turned and walked from the room, warm from his marked attention. I would do my utmost to be there, of course. As long as I could remain awake.

I had waited longer than necessary, but I needed to be sure that I would not be discovered once again. No light shone underneath the library door, and the light spilling under the study was so faint that I very well could have imagined it. I inched the door open, peering within to check the occupants before I announced my presence, but the dim room made it difficult to define what was furniture and who was Lord Stallsbury. Taking a leap of faith, I let myself in and closed the door quietly behind me.

"Lord Stallsbury?" I whispered, stepping forward quietly. Bringing my candle forth, I made out the slumbering form of the marquess beside his own low burning candle. Slumped to the side in his wingback chair, his arms folded softly over his chest and his cravat discarded on the floor, his face was relaxed, the very picture of calm tranquility. His chin had rolled forward, and I watched him a moment longer before whispering, "Wake up, my lord."

Nothing. I reached out to nudge his arm but found I could not bring myself to make contact. Regardless of my fully clothed state—though with loosened stays, for I would not make the same mistake twice—and the innocent nature of our arrangement, the one thing I could safely swear to was that I had never once touched Lord Stallsbury while we were alone in the study. I stepped back, softly calling his name a few more times until he began to stir.

He blinked his eyes awake and my heart swooped down to my stomach when he recognized me and a slow smile spread across his face.

"You came," he said.

I set my candle on a small table before seating myself opposite him, clenching shaky hands in my lap to calm my racing heart. "I did. Though I apologize for keeping you waiting. It appeared to be a hardship, indeed."

He ignored me, rubbing a hand over his face and then through his hair. He sat up taller, stretching his legs and then his arms.

"Shall we do this another time?" I asked, prepared to take myself up to bed. I was wary of having asked Emma to loosen my stays to allow me to breathe, but not remove them. The behavior was strange, to say the least, and I could not imagine what sort of explanation she'd concocted. I could only hope she was not the sort to gossip with the other servants.

"You appear to be growing closer to your goal," he said.

"Mr. Bancroft is nearly there," I agreed. "I have been prepared this whole week."

His eyebrow hitched up. "You would have accepted a proposal the day you arrived?"

"Yes," I answered without hesitation. I needed only to imagine Charlotte to remember my reason for being here. Mrs. Bancroft aside, I would do anything for my sister.

Sitting back in his chair, he appraised me. "I did not realize your affection was previously solidified."

"It was not," I said without thinking. Regret forced me to add, "I have a purpose in pursuing a husband, my lord. I have done my best to make a good choice for us, but when it comes down to it, I don't think I would be picky."

"Who?"

"Mr. Bancroft."

"No," he shook his head, regarding me intently. "You said you made a choice for us. Who is the other person?"

"Charlotte, my sister."

He nodded his head slowly, the confusion marring his brow not quite cleared. "You have responsibility for her?"

"Not in a legal way, no. But I hope it can be arranged. I don't foresee any difficulty in bringing her with me to Bancroft Hill."

"Who is her legal guardian?"

He was full of questions. I owed him nothing, yet I was not uncomfortable with answering him. In fact, I did so readily. For whatever reason, I trusted him. "Our brother. She is seventeen, though, and in need of a Season."

He nodded, though he clearly did not fully understand.

I tried to steer the conversation another direction. "Miss Thornton seems to be captivating you."

He sat quietly, regarding me through narrowed eyes. I sat in anticipation. Would he allow the topic to change? He did not seem inclined.

I was surprised when he said, "I am not quite sure that captivating would be the correct word, but she does ride rather well, yes."

"And would hold her own in a group of titled society."

"Particularly if she was *one* of the titled society," he added wryly.

"So you shall be losing your horse, then?" I asked playfully.

He speared me with a look. "I am not sure that Miss Thornton is worth more than my horse."

My shoulders released their tension and I could not help but smile. I could never dream of obtaining a horse on my own accord for my sister, but to be able to gift her a steed was more valuable than anything I owned. Even, if it came down to it, my pearl earrings. "So you are implying that I just might have a chance?"

"Mrs. Wheeler, you absolutely have a chance." He watched me a moment longer through narrowed eyes before adding, "I shall have to call the horse a wedding gift, for I do not know how else I am to explain you riding away on my steed while I leave Bancroft Hill in a carriage."

"Oh, I shan't bother riding him," I said. "The horse is not for me anyhow."

"I will not let Bancroft have him," he said with quiet force, shocking me. It was not anger that radiated from him, but pure will.

"Neither will I, my lord. I intend to give the horse to Charlotte."

"Your sister?" he asked with no little confusion.

"She is positively horse mad."

Crossing an ankle over the other knee, he leaned back with all of the carelessness of a well-fed hound.

A thought filtered through my mind and I found myself speaking before I could think better of it. "If you do not intend to propose to Miss Thornton, then what excuse do you have for setting up her expectations?"

130

Evidently, I had shocked the man into silence.

It was on the tip of my tongue to apologize for my forwardness. But this was the nature of our meetings in the study, and I would not beg excuse for that which Lord Stallsbury had, effectually, put into existence.

"Is it not my prerogative to determine whether the lady and I would suit?" he asked.

"Of course it is, but—"

"And have I not, only this evening, declared that I do not value her highly enough to wed?"

"Yes, I suppose."

He arched a dark eyebrow. "Then perhaps allow me the opportunity to *act* the cad before you so readily place blame at my feet."

Properly admonished, I dipped my head. My neck burned something fierce. He was correct, and if I was being honest with myself, I had to admit I appreciated his explanation. "Of course, my lord. I hadn't thought."

"Tarquin."

I glanced up, his deep chocolate eyes beseeching me. I yearned to say it, to have the familiarity with him that we had only feigned thus far. But I had to protect myself.

"You know that I cannot, my lord. I simply refuse."

"Why?" It was with genuine confusion that he placed the question before me. I did not know how he could not possibly guess the answer himself. If I was to become familiar with him upon any terms, it would throw into question my standing as a proper woman. These casual conversations might mean little to him, but I was not a woman of ill repute, and though I could not seem to resist the temptation to continue meeting with Lord Stallsbury this way, I would hold firm my resolve to act without reproach.

"I am about to become engaged to another man, Lord Stallsbury," I explained with gentle admonishment. "I could not, without some guilt, refer to you so informally when I do not yet call Mr. Bancroft by his Christian name. It would not be loyal and it would not be right."

An expression fell over his face and, as if by some magic, it transitioned from kindness to cold steel. His nod, direct and curt, was the only response I received, and I tamped down the frustrated sigh that begged to be released.

This conversation was not going at all like the others had.

I smiled tightly. "Perhaps I shall remove to my bedroom for the evening. It is growing late."

"It was late when the evening began. Tell me one thing more, for I have been dying to know."

I watched him expectantly.

"Whatever occurred near the pond? I do not believe for one moment that the sun gave you a headache."

I felt my face transform from tight lines of fatigue to the softening comfort of a grin. I had been wishing for the opportunity to share this with him, for I assumed he would join in my amusement, but it was not the sort of thing one spoke of in company if one did not wish to be considered a gossip. I would hate if it were to be spread about due to my own carelessness.

I leaned forward, lowering my voice. "Our Miss Pollard is terrified of ducks."

If the widening of his eyes and raising of his eyebrows were any indication, he had not expected that. I watched as his mind formed a connection between my actions from that day and Miss Pollard's fear. "You were rescuing her from embarrassment."

"That was my intent." I grinned. "And I was rewarded with an afternoon of solitude and an unintentional nap, so I believe we both benefited from the experience."

He chuckled, the sound soothing and warm like a hot cup of chocolate. "You are quite singular, Mrs. Wheeler."

Was that a compliment? His smile would imply that it was,

though the resulting butterflies in my stomach inferred that I was treading dangerous waters.

"Why thank you, sir."

"And tell me, your sister does not yet have a horse?"

"She cannot. We can hardly keep the two we do have and they aren't good for riding." My head snapped up. I had not intended to be so honest, but the words slipped free. I hurried to add, "But Miss Hurst is a friend of ours, and she has recently become engaged to her steward, Mr. Bryce. You might have heard?"

He shook his head. "I did not. But may I ask what Miss Hurst and her steward have to do with Charlotte?"

"Mr. Bryce breeds horses," I explained. "I recently received a letter from my sister that was full of praise for his steeds. I would not be much surprised if she spent all of her time in the stables and Miss Hurst was forced to drag her inside to sleep."

"You are giving me the desire to meet these people," he said, crossing an ankle over his knee. His smirk was small but powerful and I felt an answering grin form on my lips.

"I believe they are wonderful, but I am biased."

"And your brother?" he questioned. "Is he wonderful too? You do not speak of him."

The smile slipped from my face. What was I to say? I could not explain Noah's situation. It was mortifying, and Lord Stallsbury didn't need to know. Less than a fortnight and the house party would come to conclusion. I couldn't risk the possibility of rumors getting started.

But then, if there was any man whom I could ask advice and could safely guarantee would never meet my brother, it was Lord Stallsbury. And I *did* trust him.

"My brother was once my hero. Suffice it to say that he does nothing now but cause trouble."

His brows pulled together. "But your sister is safe?"

"My sister is staying with Miss Hurst. And then I shall bring her here. She will come out of this unscarred if it is the last thing I do."

I got to my feet. I'd revealed far more than I had intended and Lord Stallsbury did not seem the least inclined to drop the subject. But I was finished, and I needed sleep. The marquess stood as well, the gentleman in him likely reacting to basic etiquette. For that, I had an acute appreciation.

"Goodnight, my lord," I said. "I do believe we are resuming our tournament on the morrow. I look forward to it."

"Yes," he said, casually holding out his hand for my own.

I could not shake hands with him, that would mean we'd touch. Alone, in the study, it was not something I was willing to do. Stepping back, I picked up my candle, holding it with both hands.

"Will you not shake hands with me?" he asked.

"I cannot," I said, reaching the door.

"Whyever not?"

His soft questioning was a balm against the thunderous anger in my memories.

"I should not have you thinking me a trollop. I am defying proper convention by meeting you here, my lord, but I will not touch you. I shall do my best to remain blameless."

Tilting his head, he dropped his hand to his side. "I see. Goodnight then, Mrs. Wheeler."

I slipped quietly out the door.

CHAPTER 17

"**M**rs. Wheeler," Lord Stallsbury admonished through a grin. "I had thought you once told me you were a proficient."

I could not help but smile, squinting through the warm sunlight on the lawn. We sat at tables set up behind the archery station, a spread of tea, fruit and cuts of cold meat laid out on crisp white tablecloths. Miss Pollard and Miss Thornton were docking their arrows, the rest of the spectators idly watching as they sunk them one after the other into the target.

My own arrow had flown somewhere into the wood behind the targets, but I would have to wait until the tournament finished to fetch it.

"I believe I mentioned that I was *once* a proficient. Though clearly that talent has long since faded."

Mrs. Haley, sitting comfortably under a parasol with a cup of tea, smiled at me endearingly. "You shot the thing farther than I could have."

"Yes, your power does not lack," Mr. Peterson agreed. "I could only fault your aim."

How lovely it was to be so discussed.

Mr. Bancroft cleared his throat, setting his plate on the edge of the table. "A little more practice and you shall master it once again, I am sure."

"Unless I have lost my touch." I chuckled. "Perhaps I do not desire to master it."

"Whyever would you not?" he asked, perturbed. "We shall host a good deal of archery tournaments, I should think. I possess a prime location and it is a sport acceptable for both men and women."

My cheeks warmed at the insinuation that I would join him in hosting. He seemed at once to catch his own mistake. Until a proposal was made, nothing was set in stone.

"I simply mean," he said, flustered, "that it would be the proper thing to practice so you are prepared in the event that you must use the skill."

"If it be the lady's will, of course," Lord Stallsbury added with an air of indifference.

"Oh look," Mrs. Haley said. "It appears Miss Pollard has won."

I stood. "I shall fetch my arrow now." I escaped rapidly, passing a beaming Miss Pollard. "Congratulations," I said, ignoring Miss Thornton pouting just beyond her. I had secretly been rooting for Miss Pollard, though I would not admit so aloud. "You are quite accomplished at archery."

Her cheeks pinked, likely recalling our very first conversation when she'd attempted to convince me to allow the men to win. In all likelihood, she'd been aiming to aid her own success at the sport, though clearly that was an unnecessary effort.

"Mrs. Wheeler," Mrs. Haley called from behind me. "Allow me to accompany you? I should love to help you find the arrow."

Suspicion filled me at once. The woman did not care for physical activity of any sort. She would not choose to tramp about the woods on her own accord. I nodded consent, waiting for her to reach me.

"Do not let them bother you," she said, falling into step beside me. "You did far better than I."

"It is my belief that one's skill at archery has little merit on their suitability as a spouse. But perhaps that is because I do not prioritize sport as some others do."

"Neither do I," she agreed with feeling.

I bit back a smile, sweeping my gaze over the uneven ground. Gnarled roots sprung from the earth, blending with the leaf-strewn dirt. I gathered my gown so as not to muddy my hem and climbed deeper into the forest. The arrow had flown in this general direction, but the depth of its reach had been difficult to gauge.

"When you marry my brother, you shall come with me to London and we will choose your wedding clothes from all of the best modistes."

I tried to swallow my surprise at her candor. "I don't think that will be necessary. I don't plan to obtain any wedding clothes."

She halted abruptly. "Whyever not?"

I could not tell her I had no money for bride clothes, or that this marriage was a means to protection and safety. I turned away, searching the tree trunks for my arrow. "I do not need them," I said simply.

"You needn't be sensible for your wedding, dear. It is fine to be a little frivolous."

I tried to turn the conversation. "Do you reside in London year-round?"

She groaned. "If it were up to my husband, yes. Though I do not see why we must, for the only time it is truly important for him to be there is the parliamentary session. I often go away for a few weeks in the summer. Usually I will come here, in fact. But it is quite difficult to pull my husband from Town when there are men to entertain and contacts to network."

"He is hardworking."

She laughed without mirth. "Yes, that is true. One could not argue his work ethic."

We trailed about a moment longer when Mrs. Haley squealed, "I've found it!" and lifted my arrow high in the air.

I clapped my hands together. "Well done."

"You must know," Mrs. Haley said as we picked our way out of the woods, "your sister would be very welcome to come with you to London. Indeed, I should think it a treat to have the both of you to stay with me."

"That is very generous of you."

She preened. "You are to be my sister, you know. And we really ought to acquire at least one new gown. I should think that my brother would be more than willing to cover the expense. You shall be his wife, after all."

How had she discovered this information? I glanced down at my gown, swallowing a grimace. I supposed I had not been fooling anyone with my made over gowns. I must look a dowdy country rustic, to be sure.

We returned the arrow to its pouch, surprised to find Lord Stallsbury, Miss Thornton and her brother already gone back to the house. Mr. Peterson stood by with Miss Pollard on his arm, Mr. Bancroft waiting idly by.

"Was the arrow hiding from you?" Mr. Peterson asked with a hitch to his smile.

"Yes it was," I answered. "The tricky little thing."

The servants began to clean up the tables and chairs as Mr. Bancroft offered me his arm to lead me toward the house.

"Your sister has invited me and my sister to stay with her in London," I said.

He did not seem the least bit surprised. "How very generous of her."

Had Mr. Bancroft asked her to issue the invitation? It all felt so very staged, yet I could not wrap my mind around their reasoning. If one thing was abundantly clear, it was that Mrs.

Haley did not share her mother's distaste for me. Either that, or she simply cared for her brother more. Or perhaps she was simply lonely and wished for more company. "Her husband is a very busy man, it would seem."

"Quite above reproach," Mr. Bancroft said severely.

"Of course," I agreed. "I should like to see London again. It has been some years since I've had the opportunity."

"Your brother will not take you?" he asked, confusion lacing his tone.

"My brother is not quite aware enough of the people around him to do much of anything, sir. He could not manage a trip to London and I do not expect it of him."

He halted, spinning to face me. His eyebrows pulled together and his lips stretched tight. "I've heard nothing of this."

"It is not something I am proud to declare," I defended. I stepped forward but he pulled back on my arm, his gaze following the rest of our party until they entered the house. He clearly was waiting for privacy; aside from the servants clearing the archery equipment and picnic supplies on the other side of the lawn we were very much alone.

He spoke at last, his voice low and calm. "How can we build a relationship based on trust and mutual accord when we keep important truths from one another?"

I did not know how to answer the man. I had thought that gossip about Noah reached the ends of London's societal sphere; Mr. Bancroft's own mother had heard a distorted version of my parents' death that clearly implied her knowledge of Noah's affinity for drink.

He continued, "I cannot marry a woman who will not tell me everything I need to know. I refuse to be the brunt of a joke, and if I am not fully prepared for gossip when it strikes then that is precisely what will happen. And I refuse to look the fool."

Stunned, I merely nodded. A smile broke out on his face and he squeezed my arm where he had been gripping me. "Perfect.

Now that we've settled this, shall we go in and form a game of Speculation?"

I cleared my throat. "I find, actually, that I am quite fatigued. I should like to rest before the evening festivities if I may be excused."

"Certainly, my dear."

He led me to the base of the stairs and kissed the back of my hand before releasing me. I floated up the steps, unclear about what had just passed. A restoring nap was precisely what I needed to sort through my feelings.

CHAPTER 18

I awoke from my nap, sitting up at once and looking about me for the cause of the strange humming within my body. Something did not feel right. The fitful sleep had done nothing to make up for my previous night's lack, but there was something more. Something *off*.

I dressed quickly and left my chamber. When I found Mr. Bancroft awaiting me at the top of the stairs for dinner, sudden apprehension filled me.

"May I have a word with you in private, my dear?" He tilted his head, watching me through concerned eyes.

I nodded, following him into the study. He closed the door behind me and guilt seeped down my spine. The room looked quite different in the light of day. I was not fond of the way the sun revealed the harsh lines of the furniture, the thick leather of the boring volumes lining the wall and a hideous burgundy rug covering the floor.

In the blurry illumination of a single candle, the room had held a much more romantic appeal. The brightness was disappointing.

He stepped forward, picking up my hand in his own. A

warning bell went off in my head and I did my best to calm the swirling in my stomach, clenching my hand that swung freely by my side.

Clearing his throat, he dipped his head modestly before stealing my gaze. "There is no sense in beating about the bush. You could not have mistook my meaning for inviting you here to better know my mother and sister, and reacquaint ourselves with one another. While nothing was expressly written, I flatter myself to assume that the possibility of a union was key in your decision to be here."

I nodded, swallowing a lump of emotion. My heart pounded and a tremor ran down my body. Would he continue if he knew of his mother's threat? Or the women Emma had overheard speaking about my unworthiness to become mistress of Bancroft Hill?

"I have been awaiting a reply from your brother," he said, boring his gaze into my own. "I sent him a letter requesting his blessing on our union. But I can see now that it may be a fruit-less endeavor. If he is as incoherent as you have explained, then his blessing on our union is discreditable at best." Stepping closer, he picked up my other hand, squeezing them both, smiling at me beneath sandy eyelashes. "I admired you in London those years ago, and I have found, due to our recent time spent together, that my feelings on the matter have not changed. I would be quite pleased if you would agree to become my wife."

I blinked. The moment I'd long awaited had finally arrived and I did not feel at all how I had expected I would. Where was the overwhelming joy? All I felt was overwhelmed.

Yet, Noah was incoherent the majority of the time, and Char-lotte deserved better. I could manage Mrs. Bancroft's dislike for the sake of my sister. There was nothing else for it. I had to accept. Though I felt caught up in a windstorm, the proposal having occurred far more rapidly than I had expected, the end goal had been achieved.

Unease filtered through me as I said, "Yes sir, I would be glad to accept you."

He squeezed my hands in both of his, grinning at me with boyish joy. He stepped forward and panic ensued as his face drew closer to mine. He placed a kiss on my cheek then stepped back, relief flooding through me as he did.

"Shall we go and share our news?"

I nodded, following him from the study and into the drawing room. The entire party had already assembled, and even Mr. Pollard sat awake on the sofa near the fire.

"Would you all be so gracious as to grant me your attention?" Mr. Bancroft called. All chatter ceased and Mrs. Bancroft's shrewd gaze sought mine swiftly.

I found myself inching closer to her son. She would not hold true to her end of the bargain now, surely? It would affect her and her son as much as it would me were a rumor about my brother's drunkenness and parents' death to be spread now that I was a connection to them.

"Mrs. Wheeler has accepted me and we are to be married."

His grin was nearly bright enough to outshine any negativity from the group, but I found my own trepidation remained. Mrs. Haley squealed, crossing the floor to pull me into an embrace.

"We are to be sisters!" she exclaimed. "Now I *insist* you come to London for one gown, at least. You simply must."

"Perhaps," I agreed. If Charlotte desired it, then I would find a way to make it happen. We had not sold all of father's books yet, and Noah surely had no use for them.

Miss Pollard approached me next. "This is wonderful news."

I searched her face and found no malice. Perhaps the time we'd spent together had given her time to come to terms with the union. I was glad that we would likely be able to part as friends.

The butler announced dinner, effectively putting a halt to the congratulations. If her scowl was any indication, Mrs. Bancroft was furious and the timing of the meal was a blessed distraction.

Dinner passed in a haze, and when Mr. Bancroft expressed his desire to hear me sing that evening I nodded absently, grateful for the excuse to hide myself behind the pianoforte and gather my thoughts.

I could not shake the apprehension that filled me whenever my gaze landed on Mr. Bancroft. Visions of my first marriage and the anger which had consumed Frank on occasion were clear in my mind, and I continued to compare them against the moments when Mr. Bancroft's own demeanor had slipped. The difference between the men was simple; Frank had pretended to love me until the vows were sworn, and though Mr. Bancroft had ample opportunity to marry in the last four years, he had chosen not to. I could not help but feel that his affection was genuine.

I had made the correct decision for myself, and for Charlotte. Anything that got us out from under Noah's roof and his drunken rages was a good thing. Or so I continued to tell myself, though I wasn't very convincing.

"I suppose I owe you a horse."

I glanced up from the ivory keys and into Lord Stallsbury's searching gaze.

"Yes, you do. I expect to take him with me when I go."

He chuckled. "You shall be a fine mistress of Bancroft Hill."

If Mrs. Bancroft allows me to be, I thought. Aloud, I said, "Thank you, my lord, that is kind."

I trailed my fingers up and down the pianoforte in a soft melody, warming them up. I glanced at him. His dark eyes were clearly puzzled. I asked, "Have you come to a conclusion about what you will do?"

"Considering my reform?" He looked away, leaning against

the instrument with his hip, his arms crossed over his chest. "I believe that if I show my mother a certain degree of submission, she will put off her hunt for a wife and allow me time to make the right decision."

"That is wise. I am sorry you didn't find someone here," I said, focusing on the keys. If his mother could be mollified so easily, I saw no reason that he should not at least venture to try.

He said nothing and I glanced up after another few measures, surprised to find him intently watching me. My fingers fumbled but I covered it well, continuing the melody smoothly.

"That is a lovely tune," he said. "Who composed it?"

I shrugged. "No one. It is something I play to stretch out my fingers."

I did not look up to see if he was impressed. Instead I said, "If you will seat yourself, my lord, I am about to begin."

Chuckling, he dipped his head in response and walked away.

I was going to miss his easy conversation at the completion of the house party. As it was, I had limited time remaining to enjoy his company.

I glanced at the audience once more and then dove into my song, allowing the emotion to flow through me and into my fingertips.

CHAPTER 19

I found myself at the entrance to the study, unsure whether my presence would be well received. I was an engaged woman now, but that should not affect our meetings. They were blameless in my mind, though I knew Society would have a different take on them.

Quietly pushing the door open, I was immensely relieved to find Lord Stallsbury seated in his usual chair.

"You've come," he said as I let myself inside. "I did not know if you would."

Nodding, I closed the door tightly and lowered myself onto the plush wingback chair. "I could not sleep." Due, in large part, to my nap earlier. But it was truth all the same.

"You have had an eventful day," he said, his demeanor relaxed, his tone soft.

Nodding, I rubbed my hands together.

"Though," he continued, "you are not in raptures. Surely you are overjoyed. You are to be married."

"Do I detect a hint of sarcasm to your words, my lord?"

He smiled at me, tilting his head in condescension. "I am

happy for you, if you are happy. I was merely reflecting that you do not seem very joyful."

"It is a lot to take in," I defended. "And this is not my first marriage."

His eyebrow hitched up. "Yet it is not a surprise, either. Did you not know before coming here that you would become engaged by the party's end?"

"I did not know for certain, of course, but I was well aware of the possibility. Regardless, anticipating an event and actually experiencing it are two separate things."

He shrugged. "I am just confused by your lack of enthusiasm this evening, that is all. I've watched many couples become engaged and have yet to see a bride respond with such little feeling. Did you react this same way the first time you became engaged?"

I had not thought on that, but he was partially correct. It was an unfair comparison. Though I had believed Frank to care for me at the time, the truth was I had known my first husband for a very short time—he was an acquaintance of my aunt's—and only wed him to escape her house. Though his flowery words and empty promises did much to aid my choice, I did not realize that I was accepting a life of loneliness when we were separated and bitter anger when we were not.

However, I must have known, to some degree, that I would find unhappiness in the union, for I fretted beforehand much like I was now.

"That is the way of marriage," I said. "They are arrangements created to better both parties' station, wealth, or situation."

"And which one of them is it for you?"

I watched him a moment, his brow furrowing.

"My situation," I said softly. Part of me wished to tell him everything, but I could not. I could not tell him of the horrible anger and fits of rage that Noah's excessive drinking brought about.

"Then I suppose I must be happy for you," he conceded.

"Thank you, my lord. Though would it be so very terrible if I told you that I shall miss these chats? I do think that if my brother and I had maintained the relationship we once had, this is how we would interact."

"Can you not achieve that relationship with your brother again?"

I lifted a shoulder. "Perhaps, though quite a lot would have to change first. Do you have a confiding relationship with your sister?"

"If I did, would I be at this dratted house party seeking advice from a widow?"

I did my best not to show my shock. His remark was not uncivil, exactly, but stung all the same. We sat in the thick silence and I felt I could say nothing.

Finally, he ran a hand over his face. He chuckled without mirth, the sound both igniting and soothing my nerves. When he spoke, his voice ran down my spine like a cool wind. "I do not know what it is about you that causes my inhibitions to flee, but I value your directness. I think when the time comes for me to obtain a companion, I shall look for this very quality in our relationship."

I would have taken his words as a compliment if he had not implied that he would like every other thing about his future wife to be my very opposite. Refined, free of scandal and with a flawless pedigree and large dowry.

"You do understand that now you shall have to reside with Mrs. Bancroft always, do you not?" he asked, surprising me into laughter.

I groaned. "Do not remind me. I vow I shall discover a parish need that will take me out of the house at least once per week.

And perhaps a few projects about the house to take up more time."

"If your husband allows you," he muttered.

"Pardon me?"

"I am actually feeling quite tired. I should prefer to go to bed."

I stood, the hint received. The air in the room was not quite right this evening and it would probably do us both a world of good to cease the conversation before it grew out of hand. "Goodnight, my lord. I hope you shall find success yourself soon."

He grunted and I paused by the door. I glanced back over my shoulder and caught his gaze, his eyes like steel, unmoving.

The room was dark, one small candle on the table near Lord Stallsbury and another in my hand were all the light we had. It softened the edges and blurred the colors of the room. No harsh light brought reality to this room, which was precisely why we were able to pretend that what we were doing was acceptable.

Though I knew the truth, and whether I wanted to admit it presently or not, this needed to be our final meeting.

I slipped outside and halted immediately when a faint padding of footsteps reached my ears. I blew out my candle and crept toward the stairs in time to hear someone reaching the top and scurrying down the hall. Toward the men's rooms or the women's, I could not tell.

This was not good.

Faced with indecision, I wrung my hands together. It could have been nothing. Perhaps a servant fetched their master a hot cup of tea, or a guest came down the stairs for something they left behind in the drawing room. It was *likely* nothing and informing Lord Stallsbury would be ringing a false alarm.

I climbed the stairs slowly, not wishing to alert anyone else to my presence. My heart beat furiously as I took slow, soft steps, feeling my way along the banister and hallway in the dark.

When I made it to my bedroom, I locked the door and climbed under the coverlet, curling up as tightly as my uncomfortable gown would allow.

I was engaged to Mr. Bancroft, and there was an end in sight to mine and Charlotte's dilemma. It was precisely what I wanted when I chose to come here in the first place. So why was I not happier?

CHAPTER 20

I sat at the breakfast table watching each member of the party, wondering if I'd heard one of them sneaking up the stairs the night before. Mr. Pollard, taking slow bites of porridge, sat beside his daughter while she picked at her food with a fork and chewed small, bird-like bites. Miss Thornton sat beside her brother, the both of them with faultless table manners, straight backs and low conversation. Lord Stallsbury chatted at the far end of the table with Mr. Peterson and Mr. Bancroft, their discussion on fishing bordering dullness, and Mrs. Bancroft sipped tea with a sour look upon her face as she listened to Mrs. Haley chat pleasantly.

None of the members of the party so much as looked my way. I did not receive a single knowing glance or odd gesture. Were we to be discovered, the scandal would be great. It was unlikely anyone in the room would be able to keep themselves from casting me a look or raising a brow had they known of my clandestine meetings in Mr. Bancroft's study. Furthermore, more than one member of the group had reason to out me on the spot, for that would have been the quickest way to my ruin. But everyone sat quietly, nothing at all amiss or out of sorts.

Relief flooded me and my shoulders relaxed. The mysterious person on the stairs *must* have been a servant.

"Shall we be off then?" Mrs. Haley asked, looking about the table expectantly.

"Where to?" Miss Thornton inquired, obviously put out.

Mrs. Haley blinked, looking to her brother for confirmation.

He cleared his throat. "To Rowland Vale, of course." He pierced his sister with a stare and she shrunk a smidge, her cheeks tingeing pink. "I had intended it to be a surprise for Mrs. Wheeler, but now that my plans have been revealed, I shan't bother anymore. We discussed a trip and a picnic there last week. I went ahead and made the proper arrangements for today."

I glanced between the Bancroft family members. This was all very unorthodox.

"I have heard nothing of Rowland Vale," Miss Thornton said, her tone sweet and her expression fixed. "Is it very far?"

"Not more than an hour's ride," Mr. Bancroft said easily. "I've directed Cook to put together a picnic for us and I believe she has worked all morning to create something special."

He turned his attention on me and I tried to give him the smile he expected. "Shall we fetch our shawls?" I inquired, attempting to find a measure of joy in the prospect of an outing when all I truly felt was fatigue.

His grin was reward enough. "Forthwith."

I gathered my bonnet and shawl, sitting on the edge of my bed while Emma laced my half boots. The engagement finalized, I would now be able to properly thank Mr. Bancroft for the gift. I took a fortifying breath and pasted a smile on my face. If I could not overcome my weariness in truth, I would simply have to falsify some energy.

Two carriages lingered in the drive as the women finished pulling on kid gloves and the men waited patiently. Mr. Pollard and Mrs. Bancroft both excused themselves from the excursion, the latter citing a need for rest and the former giving no reason at all. I found myself ensconced in a cab with Mrs. Haley to my right, and Mr. Bancroft and Thornton across from me.

We were comfortably settled and the horses took off, jumbling us down the gravel lane toward country roads.

"Do tell me about your home, Mrs. Wheeler," Mrs. Haley said pleasantly, her round cheeks pink.

I felt the force of Mr. Bancroft's gaze as I said, "It is a lovely little town. Quaint, but the people are good and loyal."

"That is an odd attribute to notice," Mr. Bancroft said.

Not when one considered the dramatic event that had occurred at our last social. Poor Miss Hurst's illegitimacy had been brought to light and Mr. Bryce's aunt had arrived just in time to denounce her in the street. It had been a fortifying experience to watch and join the people who'd chosen to stand by Miss Hurst's side in the face of such social ostracism.

"I believe that my people are good," I reiterated. "Which I am sure we might all be able to say of our own homes. We tend to think of them in a grand light, do we not?"

Thornton scoffed. "I do not. Mine can all go to rot."

"Thornton," Mr. Bancroft scolded. "The ladies."

Mrs. Haley trained her gaze out her window, but I did not back down. I was no wilting flower to be frightened by one man's vehemence. Particularly when it had nothing to do with me. "I must feel only sorrow for you, sir, if that is your experience. I have very much enjoyed being surrounded by people with whom I find support and toleration."

"I can only hope that I will find the same thing one day," Thornton said, his voice low and eyes sad. "I am afraid that I shan't be long in my house now as it is, but I cannot complain of that which has come about through my own fault."

I did not ask him to explain. The implications were clear; he had likely lost all of his money due to gambling or bad investments or something of the like. I felt for his trial, whatever it might be. The cab lapsed into silence and I hazarded a glance over my shoulder at the second carriage bumbling along behind us. Miss Thornton was either wholly unaware of her brother's ruin and hunting a grand title from Lord Stallsbury, or doing her utmost to snag the marquess to save herself from ruin.

I could not help but pity her plight.

"This picnic is absolutely splendid," Miss Thornton gushed. "The meat pies were heavenly. Mr. Bancroft, you have outdone yourself."

His grin was smug, as though he had kneaded the pastry dough himself. It would have been humorous if it wasn't so outrageous. We had arrived at the vale and walked around some before settling in for the picnic in the shadows of the abbey. It was a beautiful gray stone skeleton of a building, with a grand view of rolling green hills dotted with vegetation. Birds sang above us in the trees and a vast blue sky overlooked the entire scene.

"I must explore the abbey," Miss Pollard said, rising and smoothing down her skirt. "Mrs. Wheeler, would you like to join me?"

"Very much." I waited for her to invite along the other women. Or, perhaps even Mr. Bancroft, but she waited silently and patiently for me to get to my feet. She took my arm and strung it through her own as we set off to climb the lawn toward the monstrous building.

Most of the interior had long since deteriorated, but the stone framework of the abbey remained. One imposing tower nestled in the corner of the abbey loomed over us as we stepped through the arched doorway into a wide hallway.

Crystal blue sky and white clouds stretched above us. I ran

my fingers down the rough brick wall covered in lichen and moss.

"Ghastly building," Miss Pollard said, her mouth turned down in disgust.

At least there were no ducks nearby. "I find it lovely. It is not the most beautiful building, but clearly it has a history."

"Yes," she agreed. "It is quite old."

Arguing would be fruitless. I snapped my mouth shut and followed Miss Pollard down the grassy hallway. The majority of our party was visible through open spaces where windows once sat. I pulled my gaze from them, taking in the architecture that yet remained.

Miss Pollard halted abruptly, spinning to face me. Her eyes sought mine and she spoke steadily. "I do not mean to be offensive, but I felt myself duty bound to bring this to your attention."

"What is it?"

She clasped her hands before her, glancing through the window space toward our recent picnic area. Her eyes squinted as though what she was about to say pained her. "Your acquaintance is not of a long standing with the Bancroft family, and therefore you cannot know how to interpret their reactions as easily as I can. It was made abundantly clear to me that Mrs. Bancroft is not pleased with your engagement."

Was I meant to tell her that it was a fact made abundantly clear to myself, as well? And by the woman herself, no less?

She took hold of my hand, her eyebrows drawn together. "I see that you do not believe me and I must beg you to understand that I do not say these things to cause mischief. Indeed, I have found that I am no longer concerned with Mr. Bancroft's love affairs." A small smile graced her lips. "Not when I am so thoroughly devoted to another."

"You cannot mean—"

"No!" she said, anxiety written upon her features. "Do not

guess. It is a tremendous secret and I cannot say his name aloud. I beg you will not ask me."

"You are betrothed, then?"

Her grin spread slowly, highlighting the excitement on her dainty face. "I am not. Though I will not be surprised if I soon am."

The sentiment must be returned, then. I clarified. "And yet, you cannot tell me who it is?" I glanced through the open windows. Mr. Bancroft sat with the remainder of our party on the other side of the lawn. His face was trained toward the abbey while he discussed something with Thornton. "But it is a man presently staying at Bancroft Hill?"

"Indeed."

It could very well be any of the four eligible men. I had not found Miss Pollard to be spending any length of time with any one man in particular. Lord Stallsbury stood, speaking to Mr. Peterson, before the two of them started toward the other end of the abbey. I watched them walk to the opposite side of the decrepit building before continuing down the hallway.

"Miss Pollard, why are you telling me these things?"

Her dainty face became solemn once again. "I only wish to warn you. A marriage to Mr. Bancroft includes residing with his mother. And besides that, he cares deeply what she thinks. I wonder if this course of action is wise for you."

I was referring to her potential betrothal, but evidently she was unbothered by the large piece of information she had dropped in my lap. "I am aware of Mrs. Bancroft's feelings. Do not fear that I am ignorantly tying myself to a difficult mother-in-law."

"You are very brave."

Eyeing her from the side, I stifled a laugh. Brave was debatable. I was desperate, perhaps. Mr. Bancroft was a kind man, but he was also my safe option. Marriage to him was the precise fix that I needed to get Charlotte into a place where she could make her own match.

"Now," Miss Pollard said, stringing my arm through hers, "shall we discuss the house? When you become mistress of Bancroft Hill, there are a few minor changes you could easily make. You'll want to put your mark on the home, after all." We reached the end of the hallway and pivoted to return to the front doorway.

"I should not like to step on Mrs. Bancroft's toes. It would behoove me to smooth her ruffled feathers first, I should think." Aside from that, I would be bringing Charlotte to live at Bancroft Hill. That was my first and only priority after I wed.

"Well, I shall detail my advice regardless. I have longed to recover the chairs in the drawing room. The floral pattern is far too shabby for such a distinguished room."

I had thought the floral a lovely design. I would have shared my opinion on the matter if Miss Pollard gave me the opportunity, but, evidently, she had waited long to divulge her feelings on the decorating mistakes in Mr. Bancroft's manor house. She clearly felt strongly about these fashion *faux pas*.

I unstrung my arm from hers as we reached the doorway and halted. "You go on," I said.

"You are not returning to the picnic?"

I indicated the looming tower behind us. "I would like to see that portion of the abbey."

She visibly shuddered. "I will leave you to it. It looks so gothic."

Precisely.

I turned away from her and made my way through an open archway and into the center of the tall, open-roofed tower. Planting my feet, I gazed up, watching wispy white clouds trail slowly across the opening above me. Four walls closed in the space, the open window ways filtering in some light. I took a deep breath, filling my lungs with fresh earth-scented air.

"You could be a ghost if you looked half so lovely."

I spun around, startled to find Lord Stallsbury leaning against the far wall swathed in shadows. My foot wrapped in my gown and I flailed, coming to land hard on my knees.

"Mrs. Wheeler!" he called, crossing the distance and leaning down to assist me. His large hand came down around my own and I winced. "You are hurt."

"It is a trifle."

He held my hand in his own, turning it over to look for himself. Tugging at the fingers of my gloves one at a time, he pulled the thin, worn kid glove away, exposing my hand to a sudden chill. The leather had protected my palm, but a rock had ripped through the material and my skin, causing a minor, but still rather red scrape. He traced the cut lightly with his finger, causing a shiver to run up my arm.

"I did not mean to frighten you," he said. "I told you that you reminded me of a ghost, but perhaps an angel would have been more accurate. It was not the shadows surrounding you that created the ethereal image, but the light which shone on your face."

Slipping my hand from his own, I stepped away. "You are speaking nonsense."

"I am speaking truth. If you could see the image I have burned in my mind, you would understand. Alas, I fear you shall never see your own worth."

I shook my head. Where was this coming from? The marquess was acting peculiar. "I must return to the party."

"Allow me to escort you."

I held my hand out and waited for him to return my glove. Taking the opening in pinched fingers, he slid it into place, his eyes never leaving my own. My heart beat rapidly and I immediately snatched my hand away, clasping the folds of my gown. I refused to acknowledge his arm stretched forth, instead increasing my speed from the tower and pretending that I had not seen it. His long strides quickly matched my own and we crossed the lawn in silence.

I would be thrilled to understand the meaning of the strange encounter, but I feared I never would. I would almost believe the man had designs on me, if it had not been made blatantly clear that I could never become a marchioness; I had to believe he respected me more than to infer anything less.

Mr. Bancroft's eyes followed me until I reached the picnic, his stone face studying my own. I had done nothing wrong. Indeed, I had been quite careful to keep my actions above reproach.

So why did I feel so utterly guilty?

CHAPTER 21

The following morning dawned bright and sunny, foretelling a pleasant day. The dinner party was to be held that evening and Mr. Bancroft was anxious to announce our betrothal to his friends. Mrs. Bancroft, upon hearing this declaration, dropped her fork suddenly on her plate, effectively quieting the room.

"Mother?" Mr. Bancroft asked, half rising from his chair.

She looked hard at him before spearing me with a glare and fluttering from the room. The full breakfast table watched her go in silence, before turning their heads in unison to see how Mr. Bancroft would respond.

The clock ticked three beats before Mr. Bancroft dropped his napkin on his unfinished plate and bowed to me. "You must excuse me. I should check on my mother."

Was this a pattern for the rest of my life? For Charlotte, I had to remind myself it would be worth it.

Miss Pollard's pitying gaze caught mine, her eyes widening slightly. I could read her thoughts to say, "Did I not tell you so?"

I gave her a perfunctory smile before rising myself. The

stares warmed my back as I retreated, but I found I could not stay a moment longer.

I escaped to the library, revelling in the solitude of the glorious room and the power it contained to distract me. Walking slowly along the shelves, I perused the titles, pleased to find a variety of genres. There were plenty of novels present, both classic and contemporary, and quite a few nonfiction and poetry volumes that caught my interest as well. I found a novel I had heard much talk about several years before titled *The Green Door* and curled up on the overstuffed armchair near the window, tucking my feet under me.

I became immediately immersed in the characters, scandal and intrigue interwoven amidst the Fashionable World. I was at least a quarter of the way through the book when a voice called to me from the opposite side of the room.

"Whatever you are reading must be vastly entertaining," Lord Stallsbury said, leaving the door ajar and coming to sit in a chair near mine, "for I have been standing there waiting to be noticed for some time now."

I closed the novel, keeping my finger within the pages to save my place. "I apologize, my lord. But you are correct, this book is delightful."

He glanced down and immediately his joyful grin grew taut. Clearing his throat, he tilted his head to the side. "Were you aware that my brother wrote that book?"

"Ought I to have been?" I glanced at the cover but it merely said *Anonymous*. "He is prodigiously talented. Did you enjoy it?"

Lord Stallsbury scoffed, tossing his head back to watch out the window. "I haven't read anything of his, truth be told. He is quite successful, though. He and his wife have formed a team writing books together. My mother is ashamed, but they are accepted by polite society and I don't hold it against them."

"How could you," I countered, "if you've never bothered to

read one of their books? I can only speak for your brother and not his wife, but thus far I find him quite amusing."

"So do I."

I watched him a moment longer before slipping my finger from the pages and closing the book fully, setting it on my lap. I could sense something was troubling him, and if he sought me out—particularly in the light of day—then he likely wished to speak about it.

"I have always envied my brothers," he said, his hand gripping the ends of the armrests. "The older one because he did not have to wonder what he would do with his life, for he knew from birth that he would one day inherit the dukedom; the younger because he cultivated a talent from a young age to write, and was good enough to use it to create an income. As I told you before, I once thought I might join the navy, but then Geoff died and my choices were stolen from me."

"It cannot have been easy, losing your brother and facing the life-altering change in status all at once."

He turned solemn eyes on me. "I would not wish it on any man. I grieved for my brother, but I also grieved for myself."

I did not fully understand, but I was not meant to. His struggle was out of my realm, but it was no less real than my own.

"I swore I would never become the brute my father is," he continued softly, "and I have greatly feared becoming changed by the power and authority my title has given me."

I froze. His fear for himself was my fear for my future husband, Mr. Bancroft. Could it be that they would both be realized eventually and such was simply man's nature? "Your father was a brute?" I questioned cautiously.

"Not was, he *is*. He treats his family with little care and completely ignores my mother—part of the reason, I am sure, she wishes so desperately for me to wed. She could use a diversion." He shook his head. "Not that I blame her. My father is thoughtless. His tenants are poor and living in wretched conditions, yet he refuses to take any measures to better their homes. It is a disturbing situation, and he will do nothing to change it. He cares too much for wealth; he sees not that he could be wealthier if he invested in his tenants." Lord Stallsbury quieted his voice. "My older brother was becoming more and more like him every day. I loved Geoff, but I did not look forward to watching him reach his full power. He was difficult enough to manage as a marquess with a worthless courtesy title."

I could not help but return his little half-grin. He was belittling himself at the mention of the worthless title, but it was not incorrect. I could see how his struggles were valid. I had watched my own brother alter from my playmate into a horrid drunk. His playful innocence left him and was replaced by a bitterness that changed him into an angry man I no longer knew.

"You understand," he said. "I can tell."

I shook my head. "I sympathize, surely. But my trials do not relate."

"Tell me?" he whispered.

"Trust me, it *cannot* compare."

"Allow me to make that determination of my own accord."

I let out a sigh. The man could be persuasive when he set his mind to it. His brown eyes were rich and dark and I found myself drawn into them as though they held a spell that made me their captive.

"I was close to my brother as well, when we were younger." I sighed, doing my utmost to remain impassive in my storytelling. "He went to university and found an affinity for drink. I watched him turn into someone else; all these years, I have yet to see my brother without some form of influence on him."

"You lost him," he said knowingly.

"But at least I have not lost him for good. Not yet, anyway."

"Mrs. Wheeler," the butler said, interrupting. "The post for you, madam."

I took the letter from the silver platter and sliced it open with the proffered penknife before setting it back on the tray with a clank. Glancing at Lord Stallsbury as the butler receded, I said, "Do you mind? It is from my sister."

"Not at all." He stood, stretching his arms. "I shall give you privacy."

He had only made it to the door before I had fully scanned the contents of the letter. My heart sank and my hands began to tremble. Dropping the thick, folded paper onto my lap I stared ahead, unsure of what to think, what to do.

"What is it?" Lord Stallsbury asked, coming to kneel beside my chair. "Mrs. Wheeler, you look as though you are about to faint."

I faced him, holding up the letter. "It is Noah, my brother."

He waited expectantly while I gathered the courage to speak the worst.

"It seems I spoke too soon. We may just lose him after all."

CHAPTER 22

"I just wish that you were not leaving so soon!" Miss Pollard wailed. I quit gathering the things from my vanity and turned, sharing a look of confusion with Mrs. Haley where she sat on the edge of my bed.

I had no qualms with Miss Pollard, not exactly. But hadn't she acted my rival just over a week ago? Perhaps I ought to be grateful to Miss Thornton for arriving and giving Miss Pollard and me a common dislike.

"It is only right, of course, that you should go," Mrs. Haley said graciously. "No one would expect any less. But are you certain that you won't take William's escort?"

"I cannot," I said, firmly. I was not about to let Mr. Bancroft witness the squalor I had lived in. Charlotte's letter had said that Noah had grown severely ill and the doctor recommended sending for me. That could mean a host of things.

My first assumption had been that Charlotte sent for me so that I might have the opportunity to say a final goodbye. I simply needed to get home, and quickly.

"But you will stay for one more dinner?" Miss Pollard asked between sniffles. "Mrs. Bancroft has put a great deal of effort into inviting the local gentry and I am quite sure that Mr. Bancroft would like to announce your proposal this evening."

"Yes," I said, focusing on my shiny, round pearl earrings. What would my mother think were she to see what had become of her children? "We will set out at first light. But I am certain we shall see one another in the future."

Mrs. Haley nodded vigorously. "You shall both come and stay with me in London. It is settled. When you have things sorted, Mrs. Wheeler, you must name the date."

Emma bustled past me, gathering gowns and preparing them to be packed in my trunk.

"I suppose we ought to dress for dinner," I said, hoping my company would take the hint and leave me in my room.

They did not.

"We have plenty of time," Miss Pollard said. "Have you chosen when the wedding is to be?"

I shook my head. How could they imagine that I would be able to plan a wedding when my brother was dying? Charlotte had been very clear in my need for haste in traveling home, and I felt guilt for not setting out right away. But what was I to do? It took time to prepare to leave.

And Miss Pollard was correct. I was sure Mr. Bancroft wished to make a formal announcement about our betrothal at the dinner party. I could not leave him to do so alone.

Mrs. Haley suddenly let out a muffled shriek, clapping her hands together. She looked between Miss Pollard and I, grinning vibrantly. "This will cheer you up, Mrs. Wheeler. I have heard the most delicious piece of gossip and I cannot believe I forgot to mention it before now."

My heart sped as I turned to more fully face her, clasping my hands in my lap. Miss Pollard bounced over to my bed and sat beside Mrs. Haley, her eyes hungry for scandal.

"It is being bandied about the servants' quarters that a

certain gentleman has been disgraceful in regard to another woman in the house."

"How so?" Miss Pollard asked, her eyes widened.

"Evidently, there is a gentleman who has been making secret assignations while the rest of us have slept. There is no tell of whom the lady might be—or if she is, in fact, a *proper* lady."

I felt the blood drain from my face. We had been caught out.

"Mrs. Wheeler, you look positively ghastly!" Mrs. Haley said, leaping to her feet. "I know this is distressing. I, myself, cannot fathom who would be so careless of both Bancroft Hill's reputation and the sensibilities in this house."

I nodded.

Mrs. Haley turned to Emma. "You there, fetch some tea." She took my hand and squeezed it. "You shall be much restored in a moment, dear. A spot of tea will do the trick."

Afeard my voice would break should I venture to test it out, I simply nodded once more and allowed them to administer to me. Mrs. Haley clearly excelled in her role as a caretaker. She led me to the edge of my bed before sitting beside me and rubbing my back. It was a shame she hadn't any children of her own yet.

"I can only think that my brother would be mortified to learn that this occurred under his roof. Do not fear for a moment that it was he—"

I snapped my head up. "Of course I know Mr. Bancroft is not at fault. I simply need a moment to gather myself and I shall be fine."

"Very well. Miss Pollard, shall we leave Mrs. Wheeler to gather herself in privacy?"

Mrs. Haley ushered Miss Pollard from the room, and the blessed quiet was a relief.

"Emma," I said, my voice shaky and gravelly. "Did you hear these rumors downstairs?"

"No, ma'am. None of them talk much around me, though."

Surely the other servants would have sought more information from Emma had any of them suspected me, wouldn't they? However could I have been so stupid to continue to meet Lord Stallsbury in the study? It was reckless, thoughtless, and I was ashamed of myself for putting my own satisfaction before the consideration of my reputation, or Charlotte.

Oh dear, if the truth was to become known, whatever would this do to Charlotte?

I balled my hands into tight fists and pushed them into my eyes, wishing with every part of me that I had simply slept all those nights instead of meeting with Lord Stallsbury.

"Emma," I said, rising, "I need you to make me look as respectable as possible this evening."

She looked at me through puzzled, narrowed eyes.

"My engagement is about to be announced through a haze of scandal and I do not want Mr. Bancroft to have anything to complain about in regard to me."

"Yes, ma'am. I know just the thing."

"Come this way," Mr. Bancroft said tightly, gripping my arm just above the elbow. "I am eager to introduce you to my friends."

He guided me into the room and I was suddenly over-whelmed by the crowd of strange, scrutinizing faces.

Mr. Pollard sat at his usual chair opposite the fire, his eyes, for once, alert, his confused face bounding between strangers. I could just imagine him wondering who all of these people were and what their purpose was for being here. I would have laughed at my own amusement had not Mr. Bancroft pulled me further into the room.

My arm began to ache from the force. "Sir, if you could release me," I said quietly, shocked when his eyes turned on me abruptly. What caused his anger? We hadn't had the opportunity to discuss the outburst that morning with his mother. Could she have told him the rumors about Noah? I assumed he would have brought it up had he wished me to explain.

He lightened his grip but did not let go. The butler came in to announce dinner and Mr. Bancroft said with some force, "Before we continue, I would like to announce that I have become engaged. Mrs. Wheeler has consented to be my wife."

Polite clapping littered the room and I felt my cheeks warm under the company's dissecting gaze. Lord Stallsbury stood at the back of the room, his head towering far above the rest of the guests. His gaze pierced me. Had he been informed that our secret was nearly out? Someone in this house knew it, and given the birth of the rumors, they were not doing their utmost to keep it hidden.

We moved into the dining room and I hardly ate for the anxiety which gripped me. Whether from fear for my brother's health, the potential reveal of my part in the scandal, or simply due to the rattling of the windows and thunder outside, I did not know. I had a strange sense of foreboding and could not relax.

I was introduced to the members of Gersham society who sat near Mr. Bancroft and me at the head of the table. I was relieved to find that he answered many of the questions directed my way. I very much appreciated it, for I could not string two thoughts together to form cohesive sentences. Surely Mr. Bancroft would understand if I was to bow out of the evening's entertainment. I did not know what he had planned, but I could hardly hold myself together and a full night's rest would allow my travel to be considerably more bearable.

At the close of dinner, Mrs. Bancroft rose to indicate that it was time for the women to retreat. I turned to Mr. Bancroft and said quietly, "I will go to bed now, if you do not mind. I have a long day ahead of me tomorrow."

"Certainly you are joking?" he asked, visibly stunned.

"I must awake early to travel home," I reminded him.

"You may rest in the carriage. I have only just announced our engagement. Whatever are my friends going to think if you do not stay?"

"They would likely understand, if they knew of my brother's poor health and my travels. You need only to excuse me for it to be a tolerable arrangement."

His mouth tightened into a firm line. "I will do no such thing. Will you not sacrifice one hour of sleep for your intended? I wish to make a good impression upon my neighbors and you are doing me no favors by leaving now."

I supposed he had a point. One hour could not make such a grand difference, though I hardly slept in carriages. Nodding, I turned to follow the women out of the dining hall. "Very well."

The women were gathered into packs like wolves, eyeing each other through narrowed eyes disguised with smiles. Though Mrs. Haley beckoned me toward her, I felt no sense of belonging. She stood beside Mrs. Bancroft, who watched me with poorly disguised disdain.

"I cannot think that the wedding will be anytime soon," I heard Mrs. Bancroft saying as I approached. "Mrs. Wheeler has some family matters to attend to first."

"Oh, dear," an older woman said, her white hair drawn back into a tight knot. "I do hope that everything is well."

Mrs. Bancroft tittered. "It is nothing. She merely needs to sort through things for her sister first."

I supposed I ought to be relieved that Mrs. Bancroft chose not to make good on her threat to announce to the better part of Gersham's polite society that my brother was a drunk. Better still was her decision not to repeat the outlandish claim she had made regarding my parents' deaths. Just the same, the gleam in her eye when I approached was not comforting.

"Mrs. Wheeler," the older woman said comfortably, dipping her head. Had we been introduced already?

"Yes, Mrs.?"

"Miss Ferrell," she said. "Our Mr. Bancroft is quite a prize. I hope you find yourself a lucky lady."

I nodded gravely. "Indeed, ma'am. It is fortuitous that our paths have grown in such a way that we were able to come together at this point in our lives."

"Did you not know, Miss Ferrell," Mrs. Haley said, "that they were nearly engaged years ago?"

Her eyes widened in shock. "No, I hadn't heard of it."

"Yes," Mrs. Haley continued, nodding. She seemed unaware of the daggers her mother shot out of her eyes. "It was a near miss. William was close to offering when Mrs. Wheeler's parents both died in a tragic carriage accident and she swiftly disappeared. It took quite some time before we were able to locate her, and at that point it was too late, for she was engaged to be married to a Frank Wheeler."

"You must be confused," I said. "I wrote to you and your brother, Mrs. Haley. I informed you of my whereabouts and the precise way in which to get a hold of me should the need arise." Her head tilted to the side in confusion and I pressed on. "Surely you received my letters. I continued to write after I arrived at my Aunt Mary's house. For three months I dutifully wrote to you."

Her head shook slowly. "Indeed, I did not receive a single note. I cannot speak for William, but he was rather down-trodden at the time. I assume he would have told us had he received any letters. You must know that you broke his heart."

The room had quieted some, but I could not lower my voice. "How could I have known that when I had no reply? I had to assume that you'd both moved on."

Mrs. Haley drew her eyebrows together. "And therefore, you moved on as well."

Well, what else was I to do when faced with no replies?

The door opened, permitting the men to enter the room. How horrid Mr. Bancroft must have thought me, to have left so suddenly with no explanation. He crossed toward us, his smile beaming at me.

"Is there a way that we can talk privately?" I asked. I felt I must explain. Surely he would help shed light on why he hadn't received my letters. They certainly were never returned to me.

"Not really, my dear," he said easily. "We must entertain."

"I have learned some distressing news," I tried to explain. "It would be good I think to discuss this before I leave for home in the morning."

He searched my eyes. "Perhaps later," he finally said. "First I would like you to perform."

I shook my head. "I am sorry, but I really cannot. I am not feeling particularly well."

I caught Mrs. Bancroft's scheming eye over her son's shoulder and shuddered involuntarily. She would not look so comfortable at present if she did not have a good reason for it. And that reason utterly terrified me.

"If you all could be seated," Mr. Bancroft said loudly, "Mrs. Wheeler is going to entertain us with her lovely voice."

Interested chatter rose from the crowd as chairs were moved and seats were taken. I watched my intended, my mouth slack. Had he not heard me? How was I to sing when my emotions bubbled on the surface and my mind reeled with news and implications of the past—to say nothing for the concern I felt for my brother. I was not in a good state, mentally or emotionally.

Yet, it had been announced; what choice did I have?

I slogged over to the pianoforte, seating myself slowly. I could not look upon the crowd with a smile, nor could I play any music which required a strong, happy voice.

At the moment, I was neither of those things.

I chose a tune I used to play often as a young woman, before my London come out and my entrance into Polite Society. It came second nature to me and required little strength or effort.

It was not my best performance, but I was pleased enough when I completed the music without my voice breaking.

As the song ended, silence met me. I turned toward the audience and searched their surprised faces. Stilted clapping punctuated the void.

Something felt wrong.

I searched out Lord Stallsbury to find him listening to a word from Mr. Peterson, scowling something fierce.

Mr. Bancroft, on the other hand, stood to the side of the room, his face ashen and his eyes perfectly round as saucers.

"Did you not hear?" Miss Thornton whispered loudly to the woman beside her, her voice reaching me from the sofa in the second row. "Mrs. Wheeler and Lord Stallsbury were caught alone in the study, after everyone had gone to bed." Her smile was small but feline in nature. "They were utterly alone."

I could not fathom how I was able to run from the room, but I did so quicker than I had ever run in my life. I reached my bedchamber in time to find Emma laying out my dressing gown.

"We must leave, Emma," I said, grabbing at my things as though they were a life source. "Run down and find Joe right away. Have him prepare the carriage directly."

Her eyes were as round as those on the company downstairs. I paced about the room, my heart beating as though hummingbirds flew through my ribcage.

"Yes, ma'am," she said immediately.

I grabbed her arm. "Emma, this must be done with caution and haste."

"Has someone died?" she whispered.

"Good gracious, no one has died!" Only my reputation, I thought, as I watched her scurry away.

I continued my pacing, listening carefully for footsteps on the carpeted hallway outside my door. I waited for the boot steps of a gentleman, but no one came after me. Surely that had to be a good sign.

I jumped when the door opened a quarter of an hour later and Emma slipped inside. Her face was guarded and I knew at once that something was wrong. "Tell me what it is," I demanded softly.

"You probably would rather not—"

"Emma, you must tell me. How am I to know what I face if you do not tell me what you know?"

"It is not good, ma'am. They're saying below stairs that you and the marquess were caught alone. People are saying that you and him were the ones carrying on secret *rendezvous*."

My fears realized, I slumped back against the wall. "I am ruined," I whispered.

"The carriage is ready," she said.

"But how will I escape? Surely I cannot face anyone now."

The determined set to her features was significantly more reassuring. "Follow me."

CHAPTER 23

Lights shone through windows in the small cottage when we pulled off the road. I leapt from my carriage without waiting for Joe to come around and help me out. Picking up my skirts, I ran through the mud, banging on the front door with my fist when it failed to give way.

Finn, our aging butler, opened the door and stepped aside. I must have been a mad sight, but I cared little.

"Where is he?" I asked.

"Upstairs."

I took the stairs two at a time and paused before Noah's door. The narrow hallways and naked plank floors were the very opposite of the lush home I had grown comfortable in in recent days. Squeezing my eyes closed, I shoved away thoughts of luxury and forced my breathing to calm before letting myself into Noah's room.

It was dark, a small fire in the grate barely giving enough light to show the way. A single chair sat beside Noah's bed, empty, and a tray with a bowl and cup were untouched on the nearby table.

He was sleeping, his pale face drawn and taut, dark circles

rimming his eyes. How long had his eyes been sunken and his cheekbones thus defined? Before I'd left for the house party, I had taken to avoiding Noah when I could, hardly seeing him throughout the day as he slept most of it anyway.

My heart was broken to witness what Noah had become. I could not help the acute sorrow which wrenched my heart, or the guilt that I had not tried harder to help him.

"Finn told me you'd come," a quiet voice said behind me. I spun around and crossed the distance in two steps, pulling Charlotte into an embrace and clinging to her as though she alone could keep me standing.

When I finally pulled back, I looked into her soft eyes. They had aged in the previous weeks more than they had any right to. "Tell me everything."

She delicately removed my hands from her arms and seated herself at the chair beside Noah, picking up the tray and feeding him spoonfuls of what appeared to be broth. He did not awake, regardless of her prodding, and little liquid made it into his mouth.

"Lottie, tell me. How long has it been this way?"

She shrugged. "Finn sent a letter to me at Corden Hall explaining that Noah was ill and could benefit from a doctor. Miss Hurst sent for Dr. Kingley immediately, but it appears that we are too late. Dr. Kingley told me that he's drunk himself to death. We are to make Noah comfortable but the doctor did not anticipate him lasting even long enough to see you."

I swallowed. It was just as I feared. "Allow me to take over," I said, wishing to be useful. "You go and rest."

She glanced up and I saw at once the exhaustion that lined her face. For one so young, she did not deserve to watch her brother die.

"I am sorry, Lottie. I should never have left you."

"How could you have known?" she argued. "I was perfectly content with Miss Hurst before this happened. He's ruined everything. He took Mother and Father from us, he has forced us to live in this dilapidated squalor for years with no money at all, and he has taken me from the most comfortable home I have ever lived in so that I might feed him broth and fluff his pillows." Her chest heaved, eyes fiery. "I believe I ought to go and rest, yes."

Without so much as a by-your-leave, she turned and fled.

I took her seat, chilly through my gown, and picked up the spoon. It had not escaped my notice that she claimed our brother was responsible for the death of our parents. She was mistaken, surely. How could she even say such a thing? I brushed it away and brought the spoon to Noah's lips. He was unresponsive and it seemed like more broth made it onto the bundled napkin under his chin than it did into his mouth, but I stayed at it. Surely even a little would be beneficial. And I needed to feel like I was doing something worthwhile.

Finn entered the room some time later. I questioned him on the doctor's opinions and treatment plan but learned nothing more than what Charlotte had already told me. According to them, it was a miracle Noah yet lived.

The night passed slowly. Shallow, uneven breathing filled the room, broken by one servant or another checking to see what I might need. I sent Emma to bed after she unpacked my trunk and let Finn bring me a tray for supper.

Bancroft Hill had utterly spoiled me with fine food and rich drink, and the watery soup with crusty bread Finn presented me was a bitter reminder of the change in station that I narrowly missed obtaining.

For surely the betrothal was over.

Mr. Bancroft was a thoughtful man, but no man could overlook the vast nature of the scandal that had lit fire to my heels as I fled the house party.

Whatever would this do to poor Lord Stallsbury? As a future duke, I would like to think he had escaped the scurrilous nature of the scandal. He would likely be able to skate by, though not before his name had been bandied about and trodden on sufficiently.

Oh dear, would Mr. Bancroft challenge him to a duel? My breath shallowed as I realized the depth of the trouble I had so callously fled.

Noise from the bed caught my attention and I set my bread down immediately, kneeling before Noah's bedside. His head moved away from me, a groaning in his chest reverberating from the bed.

"Noah, it is I, Eleanor."

He did not seem to notice me and turned in his bed once again as though he was uncomfortable. His eyes remained shut, but his lashes flickered in unrest. Fear rooted me to my chair and I shouted for Finn to come.

By the time the butler made it into the room, Charlotte close behind him, Noah had calmed.

"He does this," Charlotte explained, her eyes trained on him in a solemn, quiet manner. "He must be nearing the end."

"Go back to bed. I will wait up with him."

They left the room, but Charlotte returned moments later with a chair from our bedchamber. She placed it beside mine and sat, pulling my hand into her own and squeezing. It was a show of support and solidarity that placed her beyond her seventeen years. I would have mourned for her loss of innocence if I had not also been mourning for my own self.

We sat together in the quiet, listening to Noah's horrid breathing. She broke the silence, her hoarse whisper a testament of the tears that I could not see in the dim light. "What are we to do, Elsie? Where are we to go?"

I cleared my throat, sitting as tall as I could as though my fine posture would infuse me with strength. I could not mention the house party yet, nor my lack of engagement. "The cottage is not entailed," I said. "We will have to wait and see what is written in Noah's will."

If there was one, I added silently to myself. I knew that Noah dealt with the same man of business in London as my father had, but I could not imagine there was anything left to pass on. If there was, I could only hope he had found a way to pass it to Charlotte.

My eyelids grew heavy, my body too exhausted to force them open. My head drooped onto my shoulder a few times and I jerked awake, but the specter of sleep was far too powerful and I soon found myself fast asleep.

Waking up to a bright stream of sunlight in my eye, I felt foreboding heavy in my body. Drawing a deep breath, I rose on stiff limbs and approached the bed. The lack of movement beneath Noah's blanket was fortelling, yet I found my breath catch as my gaze rested on his pale, tranquil face. The still form of my lifeless brother was not a picture I imagined I would forget in my entire life. I squeezed my eyes closed, blocking his figure and the guilt I felt, for a certain degree of strain had lifted itself from my person and I did not pretend for a moment that it was not a relief to be rid of Noah's stifling, angry presence.

He was a slave to drink in this life, yet he was now free from the binding dependence of his craving.

I leaned forward to pull the sheet over Noah's face before Charlotte could awaken and forever have the pale, cold image burned into her brain.

I shuddered, the shadows that had lined his face telling a dark story I did not feel inclined to closely examine.

I sat in the still quiet of the room, the wear of the furniture evident in the light of morning. A rustling beside me alerted me to Charlotte's awakening and I put my arm around her to pull her into an embrace.

"Is he gone?" she asked.

I nodded. "He is dead."

We held one another for a few minutes before I let out a breath of air and relaxed my shoulders.

"Let us go. I will find Finn."

CHAPTER 24

The church yard was full of pitying glances and sorrowful gazes. Not many people knew Noah, but Charlotte and I had been welcomed into Linshire's polite society openly when we moved here and had gained a decent following of supportive friends. The funeral had been well-attended, considering Noah's lack of connection, and Charlotte and I had felt supported by our small community. A fortnight later, the looks of support remained numerous, but the questioning faces were more in abundance. It seemed the people of Linshire were prodigiously curious about our state of affairs.

None of them could wish to know more than I did how things would come about. I could only hope they never discovered the scandal that erupted upon my leaving of Bancroft Hill. That felt an impossible wish the way gossip traveled among society, but I *did* hope that Charlotte and I were able to settle our affairs before the truth of the house party reached my small country parish.

I looked down at the front of my gown. Perhaps I was wrong entirely and the stares had nothing to do with Noah's death and everything to do with our black gowns. Made from older gowns,

I had dyed them black and thrown them together with such haste, I was sure we looked a fright. No, Charlotte would look beautiful in anything. There was nothing frightening about her appearance. She simply had that talent. I, on the other hand, looked as pale as the ghost we were mourning.

"Miss Hurst approached me earlier to say that we are welcome at Corden Hall if we desire the company," Charlotte said as we stepped from the churchyard toward our home. "She does not want to impose upon our grief, but she has plenty of room and urged me to convince you that it would be a good idea to go and stay with her."

If there was any woman who could comprehend the fear of my situation, it was Miss Hurst. She had recently suffered a scandal of her own when the news was spread about Linshire that she was the illegitimate child of her father's false marriage. He had previously wed another woman in France and it was not discovered until Miss Hurst's debut Season in London.

I could not trust Charlotte with the information of my broken engagement, for she was sure to panic unnecessarily and she needn't manage her grief and my troubles as well. That I had successfully put off any conversations about the house party was a feat in itself. But I might find an ally in Miss Hurst. And I did long to talk of my experience with another.

"It would be good to remove ourselves from our brother's house," I agreed, shocking my sister. "I will direct Finn to start packing our belongings." What few belongings we had, anyway. There was precious little left in the house.

We turned on the road past the High Street, following the trail of doors until we reached our own cottage. We had no known relatives left besides Aunt Mary, and I was going to do my utmost to remain far away from her oppressive home.

"Shall I write to Miss Hurst and accept?"

"Right away," I said, leaving Charlotte, that I might hide

away in our shared bedchamber. Neither of us had the spirit to claim Noah's bedchamber quite yet.

I sat upon the edge of our bed, pulling a folded letter from my waistband and running my finger over the ridged wax seal. I didn't need to read it again. I had read its contents five or six times already, the sting worsening with each read. Mr. Bancroft had cited my dishonesty as his cause for terminating our engagement. Of course, we'd had no written agreement, for my brother could not be called upon to agree to a dowry, and therefore no legal action could be taken on my part.

I was not surprised, really. I had fully expected this course of events.

That did not make them easier to bear.

Though I would be lying if I did not admit, at least to myself, that I was relieved to be excused from the engagement. How I was going to tell Charlotte that I had let her down, however, was another story.

I had already written to my father's man of business in London and inquired about Noah's business dealings, but had yet to receive a reply. If it was only myself at stake, I would be content to wait patiently and determine my course of action as it came. As it was, Charlotte had approached the proper age of come out and had nothing to say for it. She deserved a proper chance among Society. For her sake, the waiting was difficult to bear.

I squeezed my eyes shut. When had life become such a jumble of difficult situations?

"I've sent Jimmy with a note to Corden Hall," Charlotte said, letting herself into the bedroom and dropping onto the bed beside me. "I suppose we ought to have Emma begin packing. I anticipate an invitation to arrive by tomorrow."

I nodded. "Miss Hurst is kind. I am grateful for her consideration, but we must be certain that we do not take advantage of her compassion."

"Of course we will not take advantage of her. Only, I cannot help but think that it does not bother her. She never seemed put out by my presence while you attended the house party."

I stilled. It was the first time she had mentioned the party. I moved on, hoping she would not inquire further. "There are many who act polite but secretly feel put out, Lottie."

Her nose scrunched up. "I feel that Miss Hurst is not playacting, though."

I sighed, grateful. She had not asked about Mr. Bancroft. "I am inclined to agree."

Miss Hurst was indeed hasteful in her request that we join her in her home. She offered use of her carriage, but we declined, for we could still, for the present at least, claim ownership of our own. Thus we packed our things and removed to Corden Hall the following day. I requested that any letters were to be sent to me directly, and Finn seemed to understand the urgency of my wish.

We arrived at Corden Hall with the sun peeking out between wispy white clouds. It was the first blue sky I had seen since arriving home to Shropshire. Could it mean that there was hope to be had for our future? I would like to think so, but the realistic part of me panicked very much for Charlotte.

"I am glad you've come," Miss Hurst said, welcoming us into the foyer of Corden Hall. "Allow Mrs. Lewis to show you to your rooms and then I shall meet you in the Morning Room for tea."

We followed the short, white-haired housekeeper up the stairs and to the right. A cat ran past my feet that we'd frightened from the shadows and I swallowed a screech. I recalled Charlotte's description of Miss Hurst's animals. It would take some growing used to, to be sure.

"We have placed you in the same room," Mrs. Lewis said to

Charlotte, directing her to a bedchamber done over in rose silk and tasteful furniture.

"Mrs. Wheeler, if you would follow me," Mrs. Lewis said, "we have prepared a room for you further down the hall."

We passed two doors before coming to a stop near an open bedchamber. It was as simple and lovely as the room Charlotte inhabited, only in a pale blue that I quite liked. Emma was already inside unpacking my trunk, and I thanked Mrs. Lewis before moving to join my maid.

The window revealed a beautiful view of the surrounding countryside, the stables to the side and a clear view of the paddock used for training the horses. Mr. Bryce, engaged to marry Miss Hurst and employed as her steward, operated a business breeding and training horses. He was in the paddock now, leading along a beautiful mare.

"You have the better view," Charlotte said, bounding into my room and settling herself on my bed. "But I believe I can claim the more comfortable bed. I received the better end of the deal, to be sure."

I leaned on the windowsill, looking past Mr. Bryce at the bustling stables and the rich, green hills beyond. Corden Hall was a home teeming with life and joy. Without the knowledge, one would not even know of Miss Hurst's scandals or the shame that clung to her family and caused stuffy older people to turn up their noses at her in the churchyard on Sundays. She was absolutely an example that I wanted to pattern myself after and I needed to obtain a private conference with her if I was going to ask for advice.

"How did you fill your days when I was gone?" I questioned, turning from the window.

Charlotte shrugged. "In the normal ways. We made some calls. But mostly Miss Hurst, Mrs. Overton and I found ways to entertain ourselves. They have a beautiful garden and a stable full of absolutely brilliant horses. Mr. Bryce allowed me use of several of them. Can you credit it?"

"I can well believe that he quickly became your favorite person."

Her grin broadened and my heart leaped. I had yet to see such unabashed joy on her face since my return home. It did my soul good to see her happiness.

Emma completed my unpacking and excused herself to see to Charlotte's room.

"Shall we join Miss Hurst downstairs now?" Charlotte asked, eager. I would have found myself jealous if I had not felt similarly anxious.

"Yes, let us go down."

CHAPTER 25

We remained at Corden Hall for a week before Jimmy, our errand boy, delivered a thick letter that had arrived at Noah's cottage addressed to me.

Excusing myself from Charlotte, Miss Hurst, and Mrs. Overton, I removed to the drawing room and closed the door securely behind me. Lowering myself into a chair near the window, I tore open the seal and devoured the contents of the letter quickly.

It was from Mr. Lynch, Noah's solicitor. He began by apologizing profusely for the delay, but he had run into a snag and had to do some research into the contents of Noah's will before he could take further action. He explained that he would be arriving in Linshire in a week's time to read and execute the will, and both myself and Charlotte were invited to be present.

I dropped the letter in my lap, directing my gaze to the front drive and the bustle of servants there. A carriage was being directed to the rear of the house and I watched Mr. Bryce walk with a stable hand, leading a horse toward the stables behind the carriage. At this rate they would need to build more stalls. The place was near to bursting as it was.

Glancing down at the letter, I read the contents again. What could it mean? The implications were clear. If Mr. Lynch needed to come and speak to us about the will then that implied there was something worth saying. If there was nothing to inherit, he would have simply informed me of our eviction date and been done with the matter.

Hope sprung in my chest. Could it be? If there was a way to inherit the cottage and enough of an income to perhaps remain there, then Charlotte and I were not destitute. We could remain in Linshire and the home we had grown used to.

A smile spread over my lips as I glanced back out the window. The blue sky spread over Corden Hall with felicitations and I stood, prepared to walk about the gardens and soak in the warm sunshine. I would grasp onto this hope with every shred of strength I possessed.

"I have missed that smile something fierce these last few weeks."

I turned abruptly, my voice cracking under my shock. "Lord Stallsbury!"

His grin was wide, his dark eyes searching mine from the drawing room door. His attire was wrinkled and his hair a mess. His luscious, dark hair. My heart pounded in my chest and my hands trembled. When had he ever had such an effect on me?

"What are you doing here?" I asked. "How did you know where to find me?"

He stepped closer, but then paused as though remembering our scandal. He cleared his throat, glancing to the window behind me. "It was easy to deduce from the village. I have brought you your horse, Mrs. Wheeler."

I shook my head slowly. "After all that occurred, surely you must have realized I would not hold you to our bargain."

"We made an agreement, Mrs. Wheeler. And I am a man of my word."

I looked into his chocolate eyes as I said the words to him I had yet to admit aloud to anyone else. "Mr. Bancroft cancelled our engagement, my lord. The agreement is void."

No surprise crossed his features and I felt a heavy weight fall upon my shoulders. The letter aside, part of me had hoped that Mr. Bancroft would find it within himself to void the cancellation. A small piece of me had still wanted to become mistress of Bancroft Hill, though I knew in the deepest recesses of my heart that a larger part had cheered when the marriage was cancelled and I was free from Mr. Bancroft's sudden mood alterations.

"You do not seem overly depressed," Lord Stallsbury said, stepping closer. He was within an arm's reach now and my hand itched to stretch forth and graze his own, if only to confirm that he was real. I glanced behind him but the hall remained empty.

I clasped my hands together before me. It wouldn't be right to touch him, though the urge to do so was almost overwhelming.

"And yet," he added, "you wear black."

He had not heard of Noah's death, then. "My brother," I explained.

He nodded, his head tilting in sorrow. The string of understanding that connected us pulled taut. "I had assumed as much," he said. "I am sorry for your loss. Though I know he struggled, I cannot imagine this is an easy time for you."

With the unknowns, it was difficult indeed. I shook my head. "Indeed, it would not be so bad if I had only myself to worry for."

"Will you accept my condolences, Mrs. Wheeler?"

He inched forward and my breath grew shallow. Could this man sense my increased heart rate? Was it apparent? I stepped back and my leg hit the chair. I was trapped. After the trouble at Bancroft Hill, I was surprised that he would place me in so compromising a position.

"My lord," I said quietly. "Please, allow me to introduce you to my sister and my hostess. I believe if we are caught alone it can do nothing but harm my reputation further and I fear for the recompense."

His eyes hardened and his mouth drew into a firm line. "Have the rumors reached Shropshire then?"

I shook my head. "But they will eventually, and this could only make matters worse."

He took a large step back. The space allowed me room to breathe, and I filled my lungs. I stepped around him, gingerly holding my breath the moment I passed his strong form. "Follow me."

He did so obediently and I took him to the Morning Room where the women still sat around the sofa in pleasant chatter, with various forms of needlework to occupy them. Charlotte noticed our presence first.

"Eleanor!" she exclaimed. Her eyes widened as they ran up Lord Stallsbury's length.

"Lord Stallsbury," I enunciated clearly, to Miss Hurst's apparent shock, "allow me to introduce my sister, Miss Charlotte Clarke, our hostess, Miss Hurst, and her companion, Mrs. Overton."

He bowed to each of the women, coming to stop on Miss Hurst. "We are acquainted," he said. "How do you do, madam?"

"I am well," she responded. "Though it has been years, my lord. I've recently had the pleasure of Rosalynn and Lord Cameron's company, however."

He nodded. "And they were well, I assume?"

"Quite well. Rosalynn brought her horde of children with her."

His smile was lopsided, the first of which I'd seen from him. It was endearing, and genuine. "Rambunctious lot."

Miss Hurst grinned. "I quite agree." She stood, facing him with her hands clasping her needlework. "Can I tempt you to stay, Lord Stallsbury, or do you go to London now?"

"I could not put you out," he replied at once. "I had intended to remain at the Crown and Ram for a day or two. I have a mind to convince your man to sell me one of his horses. I've heard a great deal about them."

A smile played at her lips. "Mr. Bryce would be delighted to show you his stables. Whether or not he sells any of them is entirely up to him."

I enjoyed the confusion upon Lord Stallsbury's brow.

And I was grateful. He must have known that to stay at Corden Hall with me in residence was a bad idea. Being here at all was a bad idea. I needed to speak to Miss Hurst, and soon. She could not proceed appropriately without proper information.

She stepped forward and tugged the bell, her butler stepping into the room not long after.

"Please show Lord Stallsbury to Mr. Bryce. He would like to see the stables."

The butler bowed, turning away. I caught Lord Stallsbury's gaze before he turned to follow the butler and my heart skipped a beat. I found I could not move, my heart pounding long after his retreat.

Oh dear, this could not be good. I clearly had feelings for the marquess. Feelings that could never be returned.

"Eleanor?" Charlotte said, causing me to jump.

I stood rooted to my place, watching out the open doorway. When I turned toward the women, three sets of quizzical eyes laid upon me.

"Miss Hurst?" I questioned. "Would you have time for a walk in the garden? The sun is glorious today, is it not?"

Her auburn eyebrows drew together, but she stood. "I would love that." Her gaze trained on Mrs. Overton, who turned back to her work as though nothing out of the ordinary had occurred. I could not risk a glance at Charlotte, for I did not want her company during this conversation and I did not wish for her to interpret a glance as an invitation. I followed Miss Hurst to the

French doors and out onto the steps, closing the door firmly behind me.

Drawing Miss Hurst's arm through my own, I trailed down the steps and into the garden in silence. I moved to turn along the path but she tugged me the opposite direction.

"Am I correct in assuming that you have something you would like to speak to me about?" she asked.

My mind flew back a few months to the time I had asked her to care for Charlotte while I attended the house party. Oh, how many things had changed in that short amount of time. I nodded. "Yes, I do."

"Then I know just the place."

She led me along a different path lined with hedges, ending at an aged, wooden door. It gave easily and we were admitted to a small, circular space, protected by tall hedges. Utter privacy, with a stone bench placed in its center.

"This is lovely," I said, shivering from the coolness. The tall hedges cut off the sun beams and I regretted my lack of shawl at once.

"Though perhaps I should have warned you to fetch a shawl," she lamented, pulling her own tighter around her arms. "What is the trouble, Mrs. Wheeler?"

Where to begin? I took in a deep breath, letting myself down on the cool stone bench. "I should have spoken to you of these things before installing myself in your home. I blame my grief for my lack of forethought, and I beg your forgiveness."

She nodded, seating herself beside me. "Go on. Did something occur at the house party?"

Had she heard a rumor, or was she merely astute? Her face did not reveal either thing, so I answered her. "Yes. I received the proposal I sought."

Her eyes widened and I shook my head, explaining, "But it has since been recalled."

She leaned back slightly. Tucking a stray curl behind her ear, she said, "It is probably best if you start at the beginning."

Miss Hurst deserved to know it all, so that is precisely what I told her. I explained my arrival at Bancroft Hill and Mrs. Bancroft's cold acceptance. I told her of my meetings with Lord Stallsbury in the study, their origin born of innocence, and their continuance—though I knew it was wrong. I explained Mrs. Bancroft's confusing threat, her son's proposal, and the scandal that had been spread at the last dinner, culminating the entire tale with my final flight that evening.

She sat through my confession with kind perseverance, flinching only when I described Mr. Bancroft's letter recusing himself from any loyalty he owed me on the basis of my deceit.

"What has Lord Stallsbury had to say for it all?" she asked.

I lifted my shoulder in a shrug, gazing beyond her to the intricate leaves binding the hedges and their unpredictable pattern. "He has said nothing regarding the rumors. We have only seen one another again just now, and I cannot tell quite how he feels about the whole of it."

"But what is he doing here?" she asked.

"He has brought me a horse." Her eyebrows shot up on her forehead. I explained, "But I cannot accept it, clearly. It was a little competition we began at the start of the house party to see who would become engaged first. It has since become nulled, for I am no longer engaged."

"But did you win?"

"Yes, but it does not count. Mr. Bancroft broke the engagement."

"Was the competition agreement whoever was married first, or whoever was engaged first?" she asked.

I thought back on the conversation in the shadows of the study and my body warmed with fond remembrance. "The winner was to be whoever became engaged first."

She shrugged. "Then I believe it matters not what has since

occurred, for you won the competition. You received a proposal first."

I had to grin. She had a point.

"If the man has only come to deliver a horse, then what purpose does he have to remain at the Crown and Ram?" she said, her expression puzzled.

"Mr. Bryce's horses, certainly. I am sure he would like to replace the one he just lost."

"Yet he arrived in a carriage with a horse tied to the back," she explained. "I watched them put it away. It seems he did not anticipate buying a horse for the return trip."

I stood, pacing the small length of the space. I knew not his motives, nor did I intend to contrive what they were. I had more important things to concern myself with than deciphering Lord Stallsbury's motive to remain in Shropshire.

I stopped, facing my hostess. "How do you receive me now, Miss Hurst? How shall I survive once this scandal makes its round to Linshire?"

"And it surely will," she put in helpfully. "I know that firsthand."

"Yet you have survived it."

She glanced at me sharply, seeming to measure her words. "You do not realize, perhaps, that it is not quite as easy as it may seem to weather such a storm. There are those who cross to the other side of the street as I approach, or refuse to sit near my pew at church. The vicar has been welcoming, and I admit that he is likely a large part of why I have not been wholly ostracized. And it has done me good to identify my friends among society here; they have provided a great deal of support."

"Mr. and Mrs. Heybourne," I supplied.

"Yes," she smiled, spearing me with a look. "Among others. The faint aura of scandal will recede with time but will not likely go away entirely. Though I have a home and will soon have a supportive husband. And I do not have a younger sister I must bring out."

"That is the trouble," I said quietly, slumping onto the bench once again. "How will this affect Charlotte?"

"I cannot know," she said honestly. "But I will remain by your side. I do not fear that your virtue has been tarnished. And we will do our utmost to not allow the prudish, judgmental set to tear us down."

The interview had not gone at all as I'd imagined. I had hoped for Miss Hurst's understanding and advice. While she delivered understanding in abundance, I had not received the advice which I so desperately sought.

I could not deny a certain level of relief, however, for it had been a balm to confess the events I had experienced of late. From the moment Miss Thornton's poisonous voice rang in my ear, I had wished to explain myself and the late-night visits with Lord Stallsbury to someone, if just to absolve myself in my own mind.

What I had not counted on was the show of solidarity.

"I cannot help but consider myself blessed that you came into my life when you did, Miss Hurst," I said, doing my utmost to tamp down the sudden wave of emotion. "And I thank you for the kindness you have shown my sister and me. It is unprecedented."

"I have had my own share of trouble," she explained. "And it was through the kindness and support of my friend's aunt that I was saved from a horrid existence at an overrun house with no privacy from my many young cousins. I am only doing as Aunt Georgina would have wished and treated you as she would have if she yet lived."

"I am exceedingly grateful."

She tilted her head, giving me a knowing look. "I am well aware."

CHAPTER 26

Three days passed with Lord Stallsbury's intermittent presence at Corden Hall. He spent a day with Mr. Bryce discussing horses and test riding a few of them, breaking for dinner with the family before removing himself back to the stables.

It was through these short, chance encounters that I had come to determine one fact: I had missed Lord Stallsbury immensely during the few weeks we spent apart and I was going to be immensely sad when he finally departed. But the sooner the better, for his presence was a reminder of how I lacked; I could hardly bear seeing the man so often when he was so far out of my reach.

Time passed like honey dripping from a spoon, dragging on. We had days before Mr. Lynch would arrive from London with news of Noah's will, and my restless pacing was bound to wear down the carpet in the Morning Room. I had convinced myself that he was bringing us good news. Whether from sheer hope or the sensible nature that he would not travel all this way for nothing, I knew not.

"Eleanor," my sister said from the sofa in the Morning

Room, "you are driving me to distraction. Can you find something else to occupy your time? That carpet surely does not deserve such dedicated pacing."

I blinked back at her. "Yes. I shall go for a nice, long walk. I have not been outside in ages and the exercise will do me good." If I could not walk inside the house, I would simply walk around it.

"Shall I accompany you?" Charlotte asked. Her nose scrunched up in distaste and I swallowed my laugh. She really did not appreciate any form of exercise that did not involve a four-legged creature. If I enticed her with a trip to the stables, I was sure to get her to accompany me. But I would refrain; a trip to the stables was not what I was after.

"The solitude will do me well." I fetched my bonnet and shawl and let myself out of the front door. My half-boots were well worn in now. The soft leather carried me around the side of the house, toward a wooded area with a lovely stream I had once ridden to with Miss Hurst. Did Mr. Bancroft regret his purchase of the shoes? I could only imagine that he would have saved his money had he known how our story would end.

I watched the clouds grow thick in the sky; the longer I remained out of doors, the more threatening they appeared. I was not yet halfway to the wood and stream when common sense dictated I turn around and make my way back toward the house. Ominous, gray clouds rolled slowly toward Corden Hall, blanketing the sky and covering the sun. I pulled my shawl tighter around my shoulders to ward off the chill and glanced about the paddock on the far side of the house with disloyal intent, but Lord Stallsbury was nowhere to be seen.

Thick silence surrounded me, evidence of the coming storm. My feet found the gravel drive that led to the front of the house and I stepped onto it, listening for evidence of life. Quiet remained. Animals were probably finding their homes and stable workers were putting away horses, leaving me to walk the remainder of the path in seeming solitude.

Wheels on gravel snapped me from my thoughts and I jumped from the path, glancing over my shoulder. Hope rose within me at the thought that Lord Stallsbury had come to visit, but the carriage soon made an appearance around the bend and I halted.

The carriage looked all too familiar and dread settled in my gut.

Whether it was Mr. Bancroft or his mother, I knew not. Regardless, I had nothing to say to either of them. As the Bancroft carriage door swung open, I was slightly relieved to see a pair of Hessians jump onto the ground and not a pair of slippers covered by a gown. Mr. Bancroft might be the second-to-last person I wished to see at present, but his mother was certainly the last.

"Mrs. Wheeler," Mr. Bancroft called, approaching me. "Your butler is not at all polite. I would fire him straight away were I you."

"What business can you have here?" I asked, disregarding all sense of politeness. I assumed, by his comment, that he had first stopped at my little cottage. I silently cheered that Finn had the wherewithal to send him on his way. What angered me above all, though, however nonsensical it might be, was that Mr. Bancroft looked so very put together. His curly hair was in order, as were his impeccable clothes. He looked more annoyed and bored than anything else.

After the last letter I had received from Mr. Bancroft, I was convinced I would never see him again. Yet here he was. I watched him expectantly.

"I do not like how we left things," he said, at length. "It was not at all an ideal situation, so you cannot fault me for my sudden reaction. But I have had ample time to consider the matter and I do believe that if we are to wed after a year's time, we may prove to the gossips that you are, in fact, worthy of my attention."

"Worthy?" I questioned. I understood his meaning, but it was not enough for me. The pompous man acted as though he was doing me an immense favor. What he did not realize was that I had determined *he* was no longer worthy of *me*.

It was possibly very foolish of me to reject this offering; I was likely never going to receive another. I could not help but hope, however, that Mr. Lynch would bring us good news. I had suffered once through a marriage with a man who cared more for himself than for me; I was not about to make the same mistake twice.

"Yes, worthy," he said with a concise nod. "Now can we go inside and discuss this further? I was told that you are staying here."

"No."

"Sorry?"

I enunciated. "No, for there is nothing to discuss. I know that I have done no wrong, and I would have appreciated your support when Miss Thornton spread the rumors about your house. I can understand your shock at the time, but you rushed to believe the worst of me and cancelled our engagement without even a proper conversation. Our ties have been severed, sir, by your own doing, and I owe you nothing. I cannot think why you want to pursue this."

"Because I think of little else but you." He stepped closer, a crazed light in his eyes that scared me. "I have been unable to get you from my mind since that first Season we met and I *will* have you for my wife."

I stepped back. "I am not interested in becoming your wife. I once was, and I wrote to you after leaving London in the hopes that you would follow me. But you never did, and that season has passed."

"'Twas my mother," he explained. "I would have followed

204

you. She took the letters and burned them for she knew of your brother's tactless decorum and did not want our families united. She admitted as much in her efforts to keep me from coming to you now. But I told her I could handle the sniff of scandal from your brother. And now that he's gone, he will no longer be a burden upon us."

I stared at the man, calm and collected with a fire in his eyes that belied his sanity. "You must leave. I will not change my answer."

He scoffed. "With everything you put me through, I cannot believe you would treat me so callously," he spat. "I traveled all this way for you and this is the thanks I receive? You are ungrateful."

"I am exceedingly grateful for the consideration you have paid me." I longed to explain that I did not appreciate his high-handed manner and apparent need for perfection. If he needed a wife so perfect, there were plenty available and willing to act the part in London.

He was clearly furious, his cheeks glowing red and his eyes livid. He turned and banged a fist on the side of the carriage. I leapt back, shocked by his outburst.

"Do not make a fool of me," he said through his teeth. "I have informed people of my mission here. I will not return empty-handed."

"That was your own choice, sir. I will not marry you simply to save you embarrassment."

He seemed to only grow angrier and I subtly stepped back again. "It is time for you to go."

He regarded me closely, his chest positively heaving. And to think that at one time I had imagined the little curly haired children we were to have. Disgusted, I waited for him to retreat.

"You will regret this," he informed me. "When you grow old, poor and alone, you shall regret this decision."

I held his gaze until he turned, climbed back into his carriage and rolled away. I could not admit until he left that I had feared for my own safety, but as his carriage moved out of sight, I let out a sigh and rubbed the sockets of my eyes with my fingertips. It was a safe assumption *now* that Mr. Bancroft was out of my life, hopefully never to be seen again.

And I didn't have the chance to thank him for the shoes.

CHAPTER 27

M r. Bryce entered the breakfast room the following morning positively giddy; the marquess planned to return for more discussion regarding the purchase of two horses.

"You are willingly parting with these horses, correct?" Miss Hurst inquired. "I happen to know that Lord Stallsbury can be very persuasive when he sets his mind to it."

This I knew, as well. Though I chose to keep my mouth closed on the topic.

"Yes," Mr. Bryce said. "I am willingly selling my horses. My intention is to build a breeding business, if you will recall."

Charlotte placed her fork on her plate with a small clank. "Lord Stallsbury is staying in Linshire longer than I thought he would." She tilted her head to the side. "Mr. Bryce, how long does it take to purchase a horse?"

"Depends on the buyer. Lord Stallsbury is thorough; he does not do things by halves."

Miss Hurst nodded her head in agreeance.

I sipped my tea, watching Mrs. Overton quietly graze her plate on the other side of the table. She had been frail and weak

207

before I'd left for the house party. While I was not convinced that she could successfully walk to Miss Hurst's woods and back, it was clear that she had gained some weight and retained something of a healthier glow to her skin. She was a quiet woman, but kind, and I was glad to see her doing better.

Lord Stallsbury returned as promised that morning—I noticed through the drawing room window—and spent the remainder of the day sequestered in the stables with Mr. Bryce. They removed to the study when the rain clouds rolled in again and remained there for two hours before the marquess accepted an invitation to dine.

We gathered around the card table following dinner, waiting for Mr. Bryce and Lord Stallsbury to complete their after-dinner port and join the women in the drawing room.

"It is your turn," Charlotte reminded me with a soft nudge of her slipper. I played my card, distracted by the idea of Lord Stallsbury in the dining room, just on the other side of the wall. His presence was a mystery, and his lengthy visit confusing. Throughout the day I had found myself quite incapable of producing a worthy stitch or reading more than a page from any of my novels; instead I endlessly paced between rooms. On multiple occasions, I had found excuses to go to my own bedchamber and watch from the window as Lord Stallsbury and Mr. Bryce exercised horses in the paddock or leaned against the fence in conversation.

Clearly, they had found like souls in one another.

"Mrs. Wheeler is quite distracted this evening," Miss Hurst said. I glanced up to catch a small grin on her lips before she laid her final card, winning the trick.

"That is plain to see," Lord Stallsbury answered behind me. I startled in my chair, glancing over my shoulder. I melted a bit in my chair from his easy smile. He caused reactions within me that I simply could not control or explain.

I had never felt this way with Frank, or Mr. Bancroft.

"Is your game finished?" Mr. Bryce asked, coming to rest his hands on the back of Miss Hurst's chair. "Shall we conjure up a game of Speculation?"

Charlotte clapped. "Yes!"

An additional chair was brought to the table for Lord Stallsbury. Mr. Bryce escorted Mrs. Overton to the sofa near the fire before returning and claiming her seat.

Cards were dealt and Lord Stallsbury looked remarkably at ease. Had he nothing better to do than rusticate in the country on a whim? Apparently not, though I could not say that it bothered me.

My foot brushed a hard boot beneath the table and Lord Stallbury's gaze sought mine immediately, warming my cheeks. I tucked my feet under my chair, crossing my ankles tightly to avoid a repeat indiscretion.

"You have found occasion to utilize your walking boots, I presume?" Lord Stallsbury asked. "The grounds here are charming from what I've seen on horseback."

Charlotte giggled. "Eleanor has walked the grounds when the sun is shining and the house when it is not. I believe there is not much else she has done but *walk*."

I shot her a reproving look before turning back to the marquess. "How did you know that I obtained walking boots? Did Mr. Bancroft tell you?"

He stared at me. "What would Bancroft know of it?"

"They were a gift from him when I first arrived."

Lord Stallsbury's disbelieving scoff rang throughout the room. "I should not be surprised that the man would take credit. But how he learned of it, I do not know." He trained his gaze on me. "Those boots were repayment for forcing you to leave your own in the mud. I sent my man to Gersham the moment we arrived at Bancroft Hill with strict instructions to procure some boots. And he did well, if you ask me."

The room was quiet. My face went slack. His sense of

chivalry was acute and I was quite embarrassed that I had voiced my assumptions about Mr. Bancroft gifting me the boots.

The rest of the party watched us in confusion. Mr. Bryce cleared his throat and asked, "You've reason to pace, Mrs. Wheeler?"

I blinked at him. If that was his attempt at steering the conversation in a different direction, it was a strange one. "I am simply restless, sir. I will feel more the thing after we meet with Noah's man of business, I am sure." I smiled at Mr. Bryce and then focused on my cards, unable to look at the marquess again.

"Yes, of course." Mr. Bryce finished dealing the cards. "There was a strange carriage here the other day. I wondered a moment if your brother's man of business had arrived early."

I shot a glance at Lord Stallsbury. Drat, he was watching me. And even worse, he looked interested. It was kind of Mr. Bryce to continue trying to make conversation, but could he not see that he was making matters worse, and not the other way around?

"It was not Mr. Lynch," I said, hoping my tightly closed lips would portray just how I felt about this conversation.

"Was it someone we know?" Charlotte asked. Her pale eyebrows drew low over her eyes. She was likely wondering why I had not mentioned it before now. Any sort of visitor was cause for mentioning. Charlotte and I did not keep secrets from one another.

Aside from the events of the house party, of course.

I waited in vain for another person to speak—preferably someone other than Mr. Bryce. When I finally lifted my head, four sets of eyes watched me expectantly. Did I look like a trapped rabbit? I surely felt like one.

I let loose a long sigh. There was nothing for it; I was going to have to reveal the identity of my brief visitor. "It was Mr. Bancroft."

A small gasp to my left indicated Charlotte's surprise but I carried on, attempting nonchalance. "He came to speak to me. We completed our business and he left again. It really was nothing."

"Then why did you hide it?"

I shot Charlotte a look, hoping to portray my need for privacy. I would explain everything to her later, if I must. But now was not the time.

"Mr. Bancroft came all this way," Charlotte continued, "and you simply sent him on his way?" Her voice was growing angry, but she did not understand. She did not have the full story.

She got to her feet. "You must excuse me, but I find that I no longer want to play Speculation. There is enough of that in my life at present. I should really not make sport of it, as well."

I did not know whether to follow her from the room or stay behind to control the damage her outburst might have caused. I looked to Miss Hurst for guidance and she smiled at me, her head tilting in compassion.

"We cannot fault Miss Clarke for her feelings," she said. "She was simply caught off guard."

"As we all were," Lord Stallsbury added under his breath. I chose to ignore his comment.

Miss Hurst began gathering the cards. "I will not do you the dishonor of prying into your personal affairs, but you will tell us if there is any trouble, won't you?"

"Of course," I answered immediately. "I can safely proclaim that Mr. Bancroft will not be returning to Corden Hall."

I could feel Lord Stallsbury's gaze warming me as I stood. "I should check on my sister."

He stood alongside me, bowing as I walked away.

It was perhaps fortuitous that I had not had the opportunity to thank Mr. Bancroft for the boots, after all.

"Charlotte?" I asked, poking my head through her doorway. She was leaning against pillows on her headboard, fully dressed. Her face pinched in frustration, she watched as I stepped gingerly into the room and closed the door behind me. "May I come in?"

The folds of her gown pooled about her feet, looking very much like a body of water above the coverlet. She sighed. "Very well."

Climbing onto her bed, I nestled in beside her, leaning my head against the hard wood of the headboard. "He proposed to me at Bancroft Hill," I explained.

Her voice was a whisper. "You did not say."

"No, I did not. I did not want you thinking ill of me."

She sat up, the wrinkles on her forehead evidence of her confusion. "Eleanor, I could never. You are my sister."

And yet, Noah was our brother. Familial connections could do little when one made horrible choices. Particularly those choices that called into question one's respectability.

Turning to face her, I delivered a strong front. At least, that was my intention. "He disengaged himself from me. I shall not go into the details, but suffice it to say that he had the opportunity to defend me and instead turned his back and ran far away. I realize that it would be wise to secure a home and place with him, but I found that I could not forget his indiscretions when faced with that future once again. When he renewed his offer of marriage, I simply could not accept."

It was a testament of Charlotte's maturity that she did not press me further for details. Instead, she watched me as though considering my words.

"I have always trusted you," she said. "I will not cease now."

Tears of gratitude formed in my eyes. I trained them on the vanity table facing us on the opposite wall, blinking slowly until they disappeared. I could not wish for a more supportive sister.

Charlotte nestled into the feather mattress, leaning her head upon my shoulder. "I suppose we now must hope Mr. Lynch will bring good news from London."

"Yes," I agreed. "Pray he brings with him a will and a thousand pounds."

Her head tilted up to face me. I grinned. Lifting my free shoulder, I said, "What? I cannot dream?"

"Eleanor, a thousand pounds is indeed dreaming."

CHAPTER 28

S un shone from the windows of the foyer and lit the polished floor. I had breakfasted too lightly, the anxieties of last evening yet to wear off completely, and my belly rumbled with the call for sustenance. Conscious of Charlotte's words, I chose not to pace the house, but instead pulled a book of poetry from the library to take with me to the Morning Room. Where, if I was fortunate, Miss Hurst would have a tray of tea.

Lord Stallsbury stepped from the study, shortly followed by Mr. Bryce, matching grins on each man's face. I moved to pass them when they halted in the hallway and bowed.

I curtsied. "I hope you have found something to take with you," I said to Lord Stallsbury. I could have been mistaken, but he looked as though he was preparing to leave. The idea made my heart patter in my chest with urgency. "I have reconsidered my stance on the horse you brought. I agree that I've won him, fairly."

"I am glad to hear it, for I've already acquired two new horses and had intended to leave him behind regardless of your acceptance."

I laughed; there was nothing else for it. "You are a scoundrel, my lord. Surely you would not press a gift upon me that was not well received."

His voice lowered and he exchanged a glance with Mr. Bryce. "I had determined to find a way to make you see reason. Now it would seem I do not need to."

There was a wariness to his tone that frightened me.

He stepped forward and I retreated. "May I speak to you privately, Mrs. Wheeler?"

I felt every fiber of my being buzz with frustration. Was he determined to ruin me forever? "I do not think that is such a good idea, my lord."

He glanced again at Mr. Bryce, who turned away and walked down the hall. They seemed to have had a previous agreement and I watched him recede, mouth agape, into the drawing room.

"My lord," I hissed. "This cannot be good. I am doing my best to act blameless and you are doing me no favors with your pointed attention."

He stepped closer still, his eyes blazing. "That is something which I hope to rectify."

Whatever could he mean by that? He turned, opening the door to Mr. Bryce's study and gestured inside with a sweep of his arm.

There was a sense of repetition about this situation and despite my better judgment, I stepped into the room. He followed me, closing the door behind him with a quiet snap.

Daylight streamed through the window, highlighting the foreign space. Lord Stallsbury stood watching me from the door, his eyes narrowed in a contemplative nature.

Crossing the floor in two strides, he picked up my hands in his own, breaking my rule against our touching and shocking me as though he had dumped a bucket of cold water over my head. I sucked in a breath, at once overjoyed and terrified over the warmth that shot through me at his touch. His hands, larger than my own, held mine with gentleness, wrapping around them like a warm blanket on a rainy day. It seemed an apt comparison. The two of us had experienced many rainy days together.

"Mrs. Wheeler," he said, "please say that you will do me the honor of becoming my wife?"

I stood, rooted to the spot on the blue patterned carpet and reeled. Could he be in earnest? No answer came from my lips, but joy erupted inside me. He had not only answered to the trouble I faced, but with a marquess by my side I would surely be able to introduce Charlotte to polite society and obtain for her a decent husband.

He must have mistook my shock for hesitation. His hands grasped mine tightly, as though with urgency. "There was quite a disruption when you fled Bancroft Hill. The family was in shock and their party soon departed. Through the disorder, Bancroft made sure to announce the annulment of your betrothal; I would not be surprised to discover that he had written to you promptly afterward."

I nodded, still uncertain of my voice. What was his purpose in relaying these unfortunate events?

"As I thought," he said, disgusted. "The weasel could not hold true to his word as a gentleman the moment scandal touched your name."

"Through my own blame," I whispered. "I cannot fault Mr. Bancroft for cancelling an engagement agreed upon false pretenses."

"False pretenses?" he said, squeezing my hands further. "There was never any secret agreement between you and I. And you very well know that nothing untoward occurred. You must at least do yourself the service of admitting that you've done no wrong."

I pulled my hands free, though it took some effort. "And you, my lord, must yourself admit that what we did was improper in and of itself. It matters little that nothing untoward occurred;

we met in private and it has cost me my reputation and will eventually steal my good name."

He ran a hand through his hair, forcing a dark lock to fall over his temple. "I do admit it, which is why I am here, making recompense. I will fix what I have broken, and our wedding will mend whatever damage has already occurred. Unlike Bancroft, I remain true to my word as a gentleman, and I will not leave you to fend for yourself."

As quickly as my joy had surged, the wave of sorrow hastily dashed down upon me with equal strength. I stepped back as though I'd been stung, gasping for a breath from the over-whelming blow.

He did not love me. He was merely proposing to fix our carelessly wrought situation. Though I should have known from the beginning. I had allowed myself to believe momentarily that he was here of his own accord. Hurt sliced through me, intermixed with embarrassment, and I squared my shoulders as best I could.

"Mr. Bancroft returned to reinstate our engagement. It was I who rejected him. And I must thank you for your offer, my lord, but I cannot accept you," I said.

He scoffed. "Whyever not?" His eyes widened momentarily as he took in my person as though through a new, shocking light. "You are not in love with Bancroft?"

I shook my head, though in truth it was none of his concern whether I was or not. Had I not just told him that I rejected Mr. Bancroft's renewed proposal?

"Then what is your reason? You owe me that much, surely."

I owed him nothing. And I was not going to admit that I had grown to love this man, not when he proposed a marriage to fix the scandal. How could I live in a marriage such as this? How could I wed a man I loved who did not care for me beyond a fondness for conversation? It could not be borne. I would not do that to myself once again. I simply had no choice.

I was not a woman prone to hysterics, but I felt the rising tide of anxiety within me and made a dash for the door.

"Mrs. Wheeler, come," he called. "You cannot be serious!"

I paused, my hand resting on the door handle. "Sir, I am in earnest. I have done so once, and it cost me a great deal. I will never again marry a man who does not return my regard. It would perhaps be best if you were to leave."

With that parting shot, I opened the door and removed myself from his presence. Running for the stairs, I sped up to my room and locked the door behind me. Throwing myself onto my bed, I shut my eyes to the world.

Barking alerted me to a commotion outside my window some time later and I rose, watching through the glass as a horse was tied to the rear of Lord Stallsbury's carriage. He stepped into view and my heart leapt to my throat. He swung onto a second horse, his face a work of stone. He called something to his coachman and was off, speeding away from Corden Hall with all of the sting of a man whose pride had taken a blow.

I slumped against the window and watched his retreat. He would survive. His lack of regard for me would aid him in getting over the rejection. If only it could be so easy for me.

No one questioned me on Lord Stallsbury's sudden departure. Nor did they inquire about my shift in mood. I did my best to be pleasant in company, but the nights were long with ceaseless thoughts of chocolate-colored eyes. Though I longed to let myself downstairs in search of a novel, I could not bring myself to leave my bedchamber.

The day arrived for Mr. Lynch's visit and as I had previously discussed with Miss Hurst, I sent a letter to Finn requesting Mr. Lynch to call on us at Corden Hall.

I had gifted Charlotte with the horse Lord Stallsbury had left behind. His motives for marriage were not in line with my own, but I could not deny that he had a kind heart. I had no doubt that the marquess intended all along to leave the horse for my sister, and she appreciated the gift with proper zeal. She took horse ownership quite seriously and had made herself absent for the previous two days. Whenever she was not eating or sleeping, she could be found in the stables or out riding.

It was the one balm for my hurting heart.

I stationed myself next to the drawing room window to watch for Mr. Lynch's arrival. Our future hung in the balance, and though I'd grown hopeful that Noah had left us the cottage, nothing was sure until we had heard what Mr. Lynch traveled all the way from London to share with us.

"Do you mind if I join you?" Miss Hurst asked from the doorway, startling me from my contemplations.

"Of course not." I gestured to the seat beside mine and heard her mentioning tea to a passing servant before coming to sit beside me. Her vibrant red hair was pulled away from her face and she moved to tuck a lock behind her ear, but there was nothing out of place. It was a force of habit if I'd ever seen one. We shared a smile before I turned to watch the drive outside once more.

"You are quite a ball of nerves, I would imagine."

"It is ever so unpleasant to have one's future undetermined," I said.

"Of that I am quite aware."

The tea arrived and Miss Hurst poured, handing me a steaming cup. She sipped her own, watching me over the rim of her delicate cup. "You must realize that you have a place here as long as you need."

I expected her to say something like that, but the reality of her words touched me more than I could say. "I thank you for your kindness. I do not think this transition would have been so easy for Charlotte without your friendship. But I fear we have imposed quite long enough."

"Nonsense," she said. "I've enjoyed the company." She sipped her tea again before setting it down and lowering her voice. "You know, I was once quite fond of social functions, when I was young and did not yet realize the depth of my father's misdeeds. After his secret was revealed, I began to dread being around other people. It was not until I came to Corden Hall that I was able to find a balance between the two. And I've come to discover that having guests come to stay is the perfect amount of socializing for me. I mean my words; you are quite welcome here."

"I thank you, Miss Hurst. Corden Hall, it seems, has been a respite for the both of us." After a moment, I asked, "Your father resides in London, does he not?"

She shrugged. "I do not have much contact with him. His other daughter created her own splash a few months ago; the last I heard she disappeared with her new husband. They likely went back to France."

I nodded, my gaze drifting back to the gravel drive in the front of the house.

"Your wait will feel longer if you sit and watch for him to arrive."

I smiled. "Logically, I realize that. But I cannot focus on much else."

She stood. "Perhaps a walk through the gardens will do? I know I could use some sun. And we ought to take advantage of it before the rain returns."

I appreciated her efforts. I would have sought Charlotte's company had she not escaped to the stables herself an hour before. "Very well, let us go."

CHAPTER 29

Mr. Lynch arrived just before dinner, to the utter detriment of my nerves. We had all gathered in the drawing room awaiting the butler's dinner announcement, when an ominous knock had sounded on the door. Mr. Bryce ushered the solicitor into his study and we allowed him time to prepare his things before he sent for us.

Charlotte held my hand, squeezing my fingers as we filed into the room. Miss Hurst remained behind with Mrs. Overton in the drawing room, but Mr. Bryce made himself present, for which I was exceedingly grateful. He eyed me closely and I had the odd sense that he knew what had occurred between Lord Stallsbury and myself, though why the thought came to me was a mystery.

Perhaps it was the pity in his gaze. Though, sadly, any number of things might have earned pity from the gentleman. Our current meeting, for one.

"Miss Clarke," Mr. Lynch said, seating himself behind Mr. Bryce's desk. He cut right to the heart of his business here, foregoing common courtesies and stating his credentials instead. "Your brother has named me the executor of his will. He has left provisions for you under the guardianship of your cousin on your mother's side, a Mr. John Wilkins. The hiccup came in finding that Mr. Wilkins has left England to see to his sugar plantation in Barbados some years ago, and I have only recently been able to locate his direction."

"He is to be my guardian?" Charlotte asked, glancing to me in confusion.

We had heard of our cousin's existence some years ago, but as his mother and mine had fallen out, there was never a connection between our families. What could this mean for Charlotte?

"Yes, he is your guardian. I have informed him of these developments. But until I receive confirmation of his wishes, I will act in his stead as directed by Noah Clarke in his will." He cleared his throat, glancing back through his papers before pulling one from the stack and setting it on top. "Miss Clarke," he said in an authoritative tone, "I am pleased to inform you that you've inherited one Clarke Cottage and the sum of Noah Clarke's possessions, which amount to a total of four thousand pounds."

My body stiffened. "Wherever did Noah obtain four thousand pounds?" I questioned, quite forgetting myself.

Mr. Lynch glanced at me and back at his papers. "He has not touched it in some years but the bulk of it is an inheritance he received at the death of your parents, I believe."

"He said nothing of it," I cried, frustration clenching my hands and gripping them tightly in my lap. We had suffered for so long when an extra loaf of bread or length of cloth would have made a world of difference. It resonated with Noah's angry, tightfisted economy that he would have a veritable fortune tucked away and say nothing of it. While I shivered in the attic sewing dresses without proper heat or light, or slaved to repair chairs and shoes long past their final usable days, Noah could have easily replaced the entire cottage and filled our bellies a hundred times over at the snap of a finger.

It did not do to think ill of the dead, but I was feeling a host of disagreeable thoughts about Noah, regardless.

"I am not privy to the motives of Mr. Clarke," the solicitor said. "I only manage his interests."

"Perhaps Mrs. Wheeler and Miss Clarke would appreciate a moment to come to terms with this new development," Mr. Bryce put in diplomatically.

"Of course," Mr. Lynch agreed. "Allow me one moment longer to finish." He searched his papers once more. "Here it is. Mrs. Wheeler, you and Miss Clarke are both to have a dowry set aside in the sum of two thousand pounds, to be paid to your husband upon the completion of your marriage vows."

Charlotte gasped. "Is that included in the four thousand pounds?"

"No, Miss Clarke, this is something quite different."

She nodded, though her mind seemed to be reeling. I could tell, for I felt a similar way. I could only assume I looked as dumbfounded as she.

Mr. Bryce stood. "Is that all, sir?"

"That completes our business for today."

"Wait," I said, stopping the men once they'd reached the door. "I've already married. When was this will created?"

"Directly after the death of your parents," Mr. Lynch said.

"Then my husband was paid two thousand pounds?"

He glanced away. "I forgot, Mrs. Wheeler. Forgive my thoughtlessness. Your husband was paid the money after your wedding. I believe I sent him the money through your aunt. Though I cannot recall her name."

"Mary." I swallowed, the dark cloud of shame and bitterness closing in about me.

"Mr. Clarke did not update the will following that occurrence, but the rest of the information remains current. Miss

Clarke is to inherit the house, four thousand pounds, and a dowry in sum of two thousand pounds."

"Yes," I snapped, "thank you for the concise summary."

He turned widened eyes on me and Mr. Bryce ushered him from the room, closing the door behind himself.

"Eleanor," Charlotte said, earnest and soft. "We shall split it evenly, of course. I could never accept such a sum for myself."

"Do not be silly, Lottie. Noah created this plan knowing that I was to wed. He likely planned the will to protect you in the event that he died before you married."

"But you have become a widow," she said. "Has that no bearing on the matter?"

"No, it does not. And besides, we know not how our cousin will react to the news. He could have other plans for you."

She squeezed her eyes closed. "I wish Mr. Lynch had not written him yet. But I should think Barbados is such a distance that it could be years before the man is able to have any say on the matter, and then I might have grown of age to inherit everything myself." She suddenly brightened. "Or perhaps the letter has already been lost in the sea!"

"Or perhaps you will wed. With these funds at your disposal we will be able to give you a London Season after all."

She could not hide her grin, and, likewise, I found that the idea pleased me very much. Charlotte deserved this. She absolutely merited her own attempt at the marriage mart. Perhaps she would even find a worthy husband on her own. If I could support her in that effort, I would not waste another moment bemoaning what could have been.

But what would Lord Stallsbury have to say for this arrangement? Surely he would have an opinion. He did about nearly everything. I shoved away thoughts of the marquess. I could not continue to wonder where he was or what he would think. He was gone.

Now that Charlotte was taken care of, I needed to consider my own plans.

Though the future was suddenly lit with a stronger flame, I could not utterly disregard the news Mr. Lynch shared about Frank. If Noah had given him two thousand pounds shortly after our wedding for my dowry, I had not heard about it. I stared at the empty desk, allowing the implications to fully settle. Though I did not want to admit it, this bit of knowledge was the final piece connecting the confusing events that were my marriage: Frank's attentive courting until our wedding, and then his detached indifference following the vows. I do not know how, but he must have known of my dowry.

Aunt Mary. There was no other explanation. She must have informed him of it. I only wish I had known as well, for then I could have guarded my heart. I felt swindled, and low. I inherited absolutely nothing upon Frank's death; I could not fathom how a man could promptly spend two thousand pounds—or however much he had received after Aunt Mary was through with it.

"Everything shall be fine now," Charlotte said, pulling me into an embrace. "We shall be fine now."

I took in fresh air, letting go of the pain from the past.

Together, we breathed a sigh of relief.

The news that Clarke Cottage wholly belonged to Charlotte and we were not about to become homeless was welcome news and we moved back home immediately. Charlotte set herself about the place determining what rooms needed fresh paint or new curtains, marking the furniture that needed reupholstering. We determined together to remove Noah's bed to the attic and order a new one to be made. The room had contained a stuffy, repressed feel since his demise and could use a little refreshing; plus, neither of us could stomach sleeping in his bed.

The summer weeks passed slowly as I awaited the news of my disgrace at Bancroft Hill to reach the small town of Linshire. Each week I arrived at church prepared to be snubbed, and each week I walked away unscathed. I did not understand, but I didn't question either. I would enjoy my continued obscurity as long as possible.

Miss Hurst began planning her wedding and requested Charlotte's and my help in choosing her gown from the modiste in Linshire. We met her on a cloudy morning just outside the shop, her auburn curls bouncing along with the joy in her step.

"I thought this day would never come," she said as we entered the shop. I reached out a hand to squeeze hers and she stopped, her red eyebrows raised. "No, really. I truly thought that I would never wed. I did not desire it until I met Daniel."

Charlotte crossed the room to look at fabrics. I had a difficult time understanding the idea. "But you must have wished for it. Do not all little girls marry their dolls and dream of the home they shall run when they age?"

She lifted one shoulder. "Perhaps, but I did not."

I followed her toward the counter and began flipping through fashion plates. She must have fallen deeply in love for her mind to be so altered. At one point I had thought that it might be Mr. Bryce and I who formed a union, but alas, it was not meant to be. I had taken one look at Mr. Bryce watching Miss Hurst and knew that chasing him would have been a fruitless endeavor.

Besides, I had already determined that I could never again marry a man who cared more for someone else than he did for me.

"Have you a color in mind?" I asked, shaking off the melancholy thoughts.

"Green," she answered immediately. "I've always looked well in green. Perhaps a soft jade?"

"Oh, yes," I agreed. "I am sure that would set off the red in your hair to perfection." We discussed the merits of the differing fashion plates and it was clear almost immediately that Miss Hurst's taste ran toward the classic look. Which was just as well, for it suited her perfectly.

While she was properly measured and deciding the details of what shaped up to be an exquisite gown, Charlotte perused her own plates and chose several fabrics of her own, all of them to her own taste.

"That is excessive," I said, looking over her shoulder. She glanced up sharply and I regretted my words at once. I was not her mother, and the inheritance did not belong to me. I had no say in the matter.

"We've done without for so long, though," she said. "And we shan't be in mourning much longer. In fact, by the time these gowns are completed we'll be nearly ready to do away with the black for good."

"And yet, do you have use for ten new gowns? Perhaps you should choose a few, and then we will reconsider the matter in a few months. By then we ought to be filling your closet for London's Season anyway."

Her grin was as wide as it was guileless and I silently hoped that our cousin would not return in time to ruin this for her. As it was, Mr. Lynch signed off on quite a sum to tide Charlotte over until he could secure written consent from her new guardian, Mr. Wilkins.

Miss Hurst spoke to the shop assistant as we made our way to the door. "Can you put a rush on the gown? I would like to marry next week, if you think that you might accomplish it by then."

I turned in time to see the shop assistant's eyes bulge. "I will see what can be done."

"Thank you. I shall pay extra, of course."

"Of course, miss."

Outside, we walked with Miss Hurst to where her carriage waited at the end of the street.

"That is rather quick," I said. "Are you prepared?"

"Oh, yes. Did you not hear Mr. Cole read the banns in church last Sunday?"

"I must have missed it," I replied. I had spent quite a lot of my time thinking on other things. I felt my cheeks warm. It was perhaps not my best moment, admitting that I was not paying proper attention in church.

"I heard it," Charlotte said with a smug grin.

I could not help but laugh. "Of course you did. Perhaps next time share it with me."

"But you were sitting right beside me," she said with false innocence.

I pretended not to hear her. "Is there any assistance I may offer for the wedding breakfast?"

"It shall be a small affair. But you are both invited, of course. Cook has everything under control and if my mother has anything to say for it, there will be quite an abundance of flowers."

CHAPTER 30

Mrs. Hurst, if she was to blame, did indeed outdo herself in the floral arrangements decorating her daughter's wedding breakfast. There was a glorious archway before the door to the dining hall positively teeming with roses that were—I assumed—cut from the back garden, and an array of flowers covering every open space inside the room.

But the overpowering smell of an excess of flora could do nothing to calm my racing heart, for Lord Stallsbury had attended the wedding with his brother and sister, and though he was not at the wedding breakfast, I could only assume that he would make an appearance at some point. Each time the door opened I stilled, forcing myself not to turn and check to see who had entered. And every time I eventually found out who it was, I was vastly disappointed.

Miss Hurst—or, I suppose she was Mrs. Bryce now—had been correct, for aside from her mother and a few close friends the wedding was quite small, taking place during the Sunday service without much festivity. Although the bride's grin was sufficiently delighted and her husband's smile equally brilliant.

I could not help but reflect upon my own wedding and the vast difference between the man I had thought I was marrying, and the person he turned out to be. My shoulders sunk as I considered anew that Frank had likely only married me for my money. I had been wholly taken in, and I had no one but my own innocence to blame.

Mr. Bryce was nothing like Frank, though, and he clearly was madly in love with his wife. I envied them their solid understanding of one another's love. It had the makings of a proper fairy tale.

The remainder of the breakfast passed quickly and Charlotte and I were soon bidding our farewells. We would not see the Bryces for several weeks while they traveled to the Lake District for their wedding trip.

Charlotte sighed as we bounced home in our carriage. "I hope to one day marry a man as handsome as Mr. Bryce."

"Perhaps you will," I said. "Though finding a man of good character would be infinitely more practical."

"What does practicality matter where love is concerned?"

I speared her with a look, considering how much I ought to share. I settled on an example that might reach her soul easier. "Do you remember Noah when he was younger?"

"Yes, though not well."

Just as I thought. "He was once very kind and attentive. He taught me how to shoot an arrow properly and how to ride a horse. He was very concerned when his friend from the farm down the lane had mistreated me and called me names and defended my honor by requesting the boy meet him for a duel at sunrise."

She gasped, and I shook my head, continuing. "They were eleven and nothing came of it, but he did *care* at one point. Vastly. It was after he went to London and found the gaming halls and friends who drank excessively that he changed. Where

Father could enjoy a card game with a drink and promptly walk away, Noah could not stop himself."

I watched out the window as we moved down the lane toward our own cottage. "During my Season in London, I was awake reading one night very late when he arrived home. He told me that he wished he could stop, but he did not know how. It had been shocking, and I'd pleaded with him to come away from Town with me, to rusticate in the country and get away from his friends. But he refused. It was only a week later that Mother and Father's accident occurred and we were separated."

"That explains it," Charlotte said quietly. "When the doctor bid me to return home, I found a letter he'd written and left on his table. It was only addressed Sister, so I read the contents, but it made no sense to me at the time."

My voice was hardly above a whisper. "What did it say?"

"Merely that it was an accident and he hadn't meant for it to happen, but if he had only listened to you and removed to the country then all would be right." She shook her head. "I'd heard the rumors that Noah was driving the carriage when Mother and Father died. I can only assume he was reckless and drunk and that letter was his apology to you."

I could only assume that he'd written the letter out of guilt, knowing himself that his end was near, and knowing that I would understand his meaning.

Yet I wouldn't have, not really, if Mrs. Bancroft hadn't informed me of the gossip that circulated about him. I would likely never know how, but Noah clearly blamed himself for my parents' death as much as Mrs. Bancroft had. Yet he had said that it was an accident.

Perhaps he had listened, after all. For he did rusticate, following their death, in the cottage he bought after selling the house we grew up in. It must have been his penance for himself.

The carriage stopped and Jimmy let down the step and helped

us from the cab. I stopped in the road and looked up to the sky. If Noah was there, and he was watching over me with my mother and my father, I would like to think that he had been forgiven.

And I had forgiven him, too.

As I moved toward the house, I caught sight of a horse tethered to a tree not far away. It was one that I recognized from Mr. Bryce's paddock, and my heart beat full hammer in my chest as I recalled the last time I had seen it—tied to the back of a retreating carriage. I stopped before the front door, stepping backward.

"What is it?" Charlotte asked, the front door swinging open behind her. Finn stepped aside for us to pass him but I could not move. Was he here? Had he waited for me inside my house?

"Mrs. Wheeler?" Finn asked, his white eyebrows pulled together in puzzlement.

I cleared my throat, glancing about me. I was sure that I looked like a frightened rabbit, but that was not very far off from how I felt.

"You've a guest in the parlor, ma'am."

Confirmation seemed to root me in place and my throat dried up. What purpose did he have in being here? My mind reeled with possibilities and I squeezed my eyes closed to block out the thoughts—both good and bad—that came to me.

I only contemplated running for the woods a moment before hardening my resolve. I had to face him. And it would be better to do so in Charlotte's company, surely, for then he would not say anything that I could not bear to hear.

I opened my eyes and jumped, unprepared to meet dark chocolate eyes and a head of unruly hair.

"Oh," I said with all of the brilliance I possessed.

"Yes," Lord Stallsbury agreed, closely regarding me. "Oh."

Clearing my throat, I avoided his intent gaze. "Are you just leaving?"

"No," he said simply.

"Will you come into the parlor?" I asked. "My sister would like to see you, I am sure."

"I have already met with your sister, but I would like to come into the parlor, yes."

I stepped past him hastily, avoiding touching him in the narrow doorway. When I arrived at the parlor I could not sit, my nerves dancing. I simply could not decipher why he would be in my small cottage. Whatever could he possibly need?

"Won't you be seated?" I asked.

He stood near the doorway, holding his hat in his hands. He gestured to the sofa. "If you will."

I crossed to the chair and lowered myself, watching him close the door and come to sit near me.

"Have you heard the news?" he asked. "Miss Pollard has married Mr. Peterson."

Now *that* I had not predicted. "That was quick."

Silence settled between us. I could handle the suspense no longer. He did not come here to exchange pleasantries, surely. I shot to my feet, moving farther away. "Whatever could you possibly need, my lord?"

"You, Mrs. Wheeler," he said with all of the comfort and contentedness of a sure man. "I need you."

I gawked. Surely, it was an attractive picture to behold, but I couldn't help it. "Whatever can you mean?" I whispered, likely as much to myself as to the marquess.

He implored me with genuine eyes. "I made a mess of things the first time, I can see that now. My first mistake was in not telling you first and foremost that I am absolutely smitten with you."

The first time? Smitten with *me*? I dropped into the chair near the window, my legs too wobbly to hold me up with any measure of confidence.

He continued, "It was not until I rode away that your words resonated with me. You had said that you would never again marry a man who did not return your regard. It puzzled and angered me, but on further recollection, I took it to mean that you *did* care for me on some level."

I couldn't nod; I couldn't speak. I could only watch him.

"What did you mean?" he asked. "Please, end my ceaseless contemplation and simply explain yourself."

I laughed, though I did not know why. My nervousness was forcing me to fidget and my restless fingers would not hold still. "I meant precisely what I said. I married once thinking myself in love with my husband. I did not realize until after the wedding that he was not at all who I thought he was. He did not love me, and he was prone to anger. It was a blessing that he was away for the war." I stood, unable to sit any longer. "And I only recently discovered that he married me for my dowry. Though how he learned of it when I myself knew nothing of it is a mystery."

"Likely from your aunt," Lord Stallsbury said at once. "I know her but was never fond of the woman so I chose to say nothing about our acquaintance. We do not live very far from one another, though our circles do not mix often. She is a sniveling, selfish woman and would sell her own child for gain. I am sure she found a way to make a deal with your husband to get you married so quickly."

I did not recall telling Lord Stallsbury anything about myself or the timeline of my wedding. He must have inquired on his own. I was unsure if the concept bothered me or not; I only felt strange. "There is simply too much to understand."

"I know," he agreed, coming to stand near me in the bright sunlight of the front facing window. He did not attempt to touch me, for which I was eternally grateful. He was respecting my boundaries as he often had in the study at Bancroft Hill, gentleman that he was. When he spoke again his voice was low and steady. It captured me, compelling me to gaze at him. "There is a lot to take in at the moment, but the most important thing is that I love you, Eleanor. I love you dearly. I tried to forget you, to respect the distance you requested, but I found that I could not. It has been made abundantly clear to me in the course of the previous month that I very well cannot live without you."

Tears smarted in my eyes and I blinked rapidly to push them away. It was a pretty speech, and the sheen in his own gaze was proof enough that he meant his words.

"And," he continued, lowering his voice and stepping closer, "I would be lying if I did not mention that I long to hear you sing again."

I laughed at the absurdity of his statement.

"I should be a happy man if I can hear your angelic voice for the rest of my days, for then I should *truly* have won."

"I already won," I reminded him, "and I have your horse outside to prove it."

"That horse is Charlotte's now. And if you agree to be my wife, then it is I who have won the finest prize of all."

"My voice?" I inquired.

"No, darling. Your heart."

There was nothing for it; I simply had to lean forward and kiss him.

Clapping met us at once and I jumped away from him, turning my hot cheeks toward the doorway to find Charlotte grinning there. "That was a pretty speech," she said.

"Lottie, please leave," I begged.

"But you have not even answered him," she protested.

He grinned. "She is correct, you know."

Turning my smile back toward the man that I loved, deeply, I said, "Yes, my lord, I shall marry you."

"*Tarquin*, if you please."

I could not help but grin. "Very well, Tarquin."

His answering smile was short lived as he pulled me close and kissed me hard. My hands found the lapels of his coat and grasped them, holding on for dear life.

I'd never finished reading my gothic novel about the highwayman-turned-earl, but now I didn't need to. My own highwayman ended up being enough of a happily ever after for me.

EPILOGUE

"Mr. Thornton, you've received a letter."

Sighing, I slapped the cards on the playing table, turning frustrated eyes on my butler, Melville. Could he not see that I was in the middle of an important game? One more hand in my favor and I would win enough to pay off my vowels to Mr. James. I took the letter, requesting Melville to bring more ale.

"My apologies," I said to Mr. James, flipping the letter to see who it was from. Lord Stallsbury. I could get to it later. I tossed it aside and turned my attention to the man across from me.

His eyes were sharp for a man so old. Particularly when considering how much he'd had to drink that evening.

Melville returned with more ale and we waited for him to leave before playing once more. I filled my glass, downing half the contents quickly. We flipped our cards and the drink sank to the bottom of my stomach, souring. I clamped my mouth shut. How would I recover from this?

"One more game?" I asked, hoping to sound nonchalant.

Mr. James scoffed, tossing his cards to the table. "You've nothing left to wager, boy."

My eyes immediately sought the painting hanging on the opposite wall, over the older man's white head of hair. My summer house, Thornville. Sarah would be livid. But what else could I do? We couldn't very well pay all of my debts with the sale of the house anyway.

Either way, we were sunk.

"Perhaps I do."

I'd grabbed his attention. He glanced at me under bushy white eyebrows, his side whiskers twitching while he chewed on his cheek. "What is it?"

"Thornville."

He stilled, and I tried not to show my nerves.

"You're serious, Thornton?"

I nodded.

"What's the wager?" he asked.

"The house, for all of my debts."

"Deal."

I shook my head. "*All* of my debts, James. If I win, you pay off everything. If you win, you get my house."

The older man tried to contain his smile and I knew I had him.

"Deal," he said, this time with more pleasure.

A warning rang through my body but I paid it no heed. The ale had done nothing to blur my sensibilities, for I had drank a tenth of what I'd poured this evening for my friend. I could not find my practices unethical, for they were no worse than what I'd find in any gaming house in all of London.

The cards were shuffled and dealt, and there was a nervous energy about us as we played. My hopes rose with each new card and I found my heart beating a rapid succession in my chest. I'd dug this hole myself, but I was about to get Sarah and I out of this mess once and for all. It was time to quit the cards and focus on my estate. Once my debts were paid, that is.

I watched Mr. James check his cards, a slight twitch to his

mouth that I'd come to learn was his tell. I froze, unsure if he was eager or displeased by what he'd drawn. Swallowing, I laid my cards face up, my breath shallow and infused with equal parts fear and excitement.

Mr. James locked eyes with me. "Your life is about to change, Thornton."

He laid his cards and my world spun.

That was certainly an understatement. I let out a breath and closed my eyes. It was a done deal now, and there was no turning back.

About the Author

Kasey Stockton is a staunch lover of all things romantic. She doesn't discriminate between genres and enjoys a wide variety of happily ever afters. Drawn to the Regency period at a young age when gifted a copy of *Sense and Sensibility* by her grandmother, Kasey initially began writing Regency romances. She has since written in a variety of genres, but all of her titles fall under clean romance. A native of northern California, she now resides in Texas with her own prince charming and their three children. When not reading, writing, or binge-watching chick flicks, she enjoys running, cutting hair, and anything chocolate.

Made in the USA
Monee, IL
09 July 2024

61568941R00146